DIMENSION X

"Your intelligence was bred out. It is gone.
Children that should have been born never were.
The just-average, they'll-get-along majority took
over the population. The average IQ now is 45."
"But that's far in the future—"
"So are you," grunted the hawk-faced man sourly.
"But who are *you* people?"
"Just people—real people. Some generations ago,
the geneticists realized at last that nobody was
going to pay any attention to what they said, so
they abandoned words for deeds. Specifically,
they formed and recruited for a closed
corporation intended to maintain and improve
the breed. We are their descendants, about three
million of us. There are five billion of the others,
so we are their slaves."

Dimension X

TWO NOVELLAS
EDITED BY

Damon Knight

CORONET BOOKS
Hodder Fawcett Ltd., London

Copyright © 1970 by Damon Knight
First published by Victor Gollancz Ltd, 1970
Coronet edition 1974

This book was originally published in one volume
with the stories contained in *Elsewhere* × 3.

Printed in Great Britain
for Coronet Books, Hodder Fawcett Ltd.,
St Paul's House, Warwick Lane, London, EC4P 4AH,
by Richard Clay (The Chaucer Press), Ltd.,
Bungay, Suffolk.

ISBN 0 340 16787 4

CONTENTS

ACKNOWLEDGMENTS

'The Man Who Sold the Moon', by Robert A. Heinlein, copyright 1949 by Robert A. Heinlein; reprinted from *The Man Who Sold the Moon* by permission of the author and Lurton Blassingame.

'The Marching Morons', by C. M. Kornbluth, copyright 1951 by Galaxy Publishing Corp.; reprinted from *Galaxy* by permission of Robert P. Mills, Ltd.

The Man Who Sold the Moon

The Man Who Sold the Moon

ROBERT A. HEINLEIN

In 1949, when this story was first published, a flight to the Moon was science fiction—or, as most people still called it, "pseudoscience." In 1969, as I write, it is journalism. The curious thing is that Heinlein's account does not suffer by contrast with the "real" events as they actually happen. His fiction is so circumstantial, so believable, and so self-consistent that it has a reality of its own.

"The Man Who Sold the Moon" is the story of a man obsessed by a private vision. Ordinary people can't cope with him because they are limited by prudence and common sense. They fear him, admire him in spite of themselves, and in the end bring him down; but it is his vision, not theirs, that shapes the world they will have to live in. All this is precisely observed, profoundly true, even though it "never happened": it is true in the sense that the story of Moses and the Promised Land is true.

Y̶ou've got to be a believer!"

George Strong snorted at his partner's declaration. "Delos, why don't you give up? You've been singing this tune for years. Maybe someday men will get to the Moon, though I doubt it. In any case, you and I will never live to see it. The loss of the power satellite washes the matter up for our generation."

D. D. Harriman grunted. "We won't see it if we sit on our fat behinds and don't do anything to make it happen. But we can make it happen."

"Question number one: how? Question number two: why?"

" 'Why?' The man asks 'why.' George, isn't there anything in your soul but discounts and dividends? Didn't you ever sit with a girl on a soft summer night and stare up at the Moon and wonder what was there?"

"Yeah, I did once. I caught a cold."

Harriman asked the Almighty why he had been delivered into the hands of the Philistines. He then turned back to his partner. "I could tell you why, the real 'why,' but you wouldn't understand me. You want to know why in terms of cash, don't you? You want to know how Harriman & Strong and Harriman Enterprises can show a profit, don't you?"

"Yes," admitted Strong, "and don't give me any guff about tourist trade and fabulous lunar jewels. I've had it."

"You ask me to show figures on a brand-new type of enterprise, knowing I can't. It's like asking the Wright brothers at Kitty Hawk to estimate how much money Curtiss-Wright Corporation would someday make out of building airplanes. I'll put it another way. You didn't want us to go into plastic houses, did you? If you had had your way we would still be back in Kansas City, subdividing cow pastures and showing rentals."

Strong shrugged.

"How much has New World Homes made to date?"

Strong looked absentminded while exercising the talent he brought to the partnership. "Uh . . . $172,946,004.62, after taxes, to the end of the last fiscal year. The running estimate to date is—"

"Never mind. What was our share in the take?"

"Well, uh, the partnership, exclusive of the piece you took personally and then sold to me later, has benefited from New World Homes during the same period by $13,010,437.20, ahead of personal taxes. Delos, this double taxation has got to stop. Penalizing thrift is a sure way to run this country straight into—"

"Forget it, forget it! How much have we made out of Skyblast Freight and Antipodes Transways?"

Strong told him.

"And yet I had to threaten you with bodily harm to get you to put up a dime to buy control of the injector patent. You said rockets were a passing fad."

"We were lucky," objected Strong. "You had no way of knowing that there would be a big uranium strike in Australia. Without it, the Skyways group would have left us in the red. For that matter New World Homes would have failed, too, if the roadtowns hadn't come along and given us a market out from under local building codes."

"Nuts on both points. Fast transportation will pay; it always has. As for New World, when ten million families need new houses and we can sell 'em cheap, they'll buy. They won't let building codes stop them, not permanently. We gambled on a certainty. Think back, George: what ventures have we lost money on and what ones have paid off? Every one of my crackbrain ideas has made money, hasn't it? And the only times we've lost our ante was on conservative, blue-chip investments."

"But we've made money on some conservative deals, too," protested Strong.

"Not enough to pay for your yacht. Be fair about it, George; the Andes Development Company, the integrating pantograph patent, every one of my wildcat schemes I've had to drag you into—and every one of them paid."

"I've had to sweat blood to make them pay," Strong grumbled.

"That's why we are partners. I get a wildcat by the tail; you harness him and put him to work. Now we go to the Moon—and you'll make it pay."

"Speak for yourself. I'm not going to the Moon."

"I am."

"Hummph! Delos, granting that we have gotten rich by speculating on your hunches, it's a steel-clad fact that if you keep on gambling you lose your shirt. There's an old saw about the pitcher that went once too often to the well."

"Damn it, George—I'm going to the Moon! If you won't back me up, let's liquidate and I'll do it alone."

Strong drummed on his desk top. "Now, Delos, nobody said anything about not backing you up."

"Fish or cut bait. Now is the opportunity and my mind's made up. I'm going to be the Man in the Moon."

"Well . . . let's get going. We'll be late to the meeting."

As they left their joint office, Strong, always penny conscious, was careful to switch off the light. Harriman had seen him do so a thousand times; this time he commented. "George, how about a light switch that turns off automatically when you leave a room?"

"Hmm—but suppose someone were left in the room?"

"Well . . . hitch it to stay on only when someone was *in* the room—key the switch to the human body's heat radiation, maybe."

"Too expensive and too complicated."

"Needn't be. I'll turn the idea over to Ferguson to fiddle with. It should be no larger than the present light switch and cheap enough so that the power saved in a year will pay for it."

"How would it work?" asked Strong.

"How should I know? I'm no engineer; that's for Ferguson and the other educated laddies."

Strong objected, "It's no good commercially. Switching off a light when you leave a room is a matter of temperament. I've got it; you haven't. If a man hasn't got it, you can't interest him in such a switch."

"You can if power continues to be rationed. There is a power shortage now; and there will be a bigger one."

"Just temporary. This meeting will straighten it out."

"George, there is nothing in this world so permanent as a temporary emergency. The switch will sell."

Strong took out a notebook and stylus. "I'll call Ferguson in about it tomorrow."

Harriman forgot the matter, never to think of it again. They had reached the roof; he waved to a taxi, then turned to Strong. "How much could we realize if we unloaded our holdings in Roadways and in Belt Transport Corporation—yes, and in New World Homes?"

"Huh? Have you gone crazy?"

"Probably. But I'm going to need all the cash you can shake loose for me. Roadways and Belt Transport are no good anyhow; we should have unloaded earlier."

"You *are* crazy! It's the one really conservative venture you've sponsored."

"But it wasn't conservative when I sponsored it. Believe me, George, roadtowns are on their way out. They are growing moribund, just as the railroads did. In a hundred years there won't be a one left on the continent. What's the formula for making money, George?"

"Buy low and sell high."

"That's only half of it . . . *your* half. We've got to guess which way things are moving, give them a boost, and see that we are cut in on the ground floor. Liquidate that stuff, George; I'll need money to operate." The taxi landed; they got in and took off.

The taxi delivered them to the roof of the Hemisphere Power Building; they went to the power syndicate's board room, as far below ground as the landing platform was above—in those days, despite years of peace, tycoons habitually came to rest at spots relatively immune to atom bombs. The room did not seem like a bomb shelter; it appeared to be a chamber in a luxurious penthouse, for a "view window" back of the chairman's end of the table looked out high above the city, in convincing, live stereo, relayed from the roof.

The other directors were there before them. Dixon nodded as they came in, glanced at his watch finger and said, "Well, gentlemen, our bad boy is here, we may as well begin." He took the chairman's seat and rapped for order.

"The minutes of the last meeting are on your pads as usual. Signal when ready." Harriman glanced at the summary before him and at once flipped a switch on the tabletop; a small green light flashed on at his place. Most of the directors did the same.

"Who's holding up the procession?" inquired Harriman, looking around. "Oh—you, George. Get a move on."

"I like to check the figures," his partner answered testily, then flipped his own switch. A larger green light showed in front of Chairman Dixon, who then pressed a button; a transparency, sticking an inch or two above the tabletop in front of him, lit up with the word RECORDING.

"Operations report," said Dixon and touched another switch. A female voice came out from nowhere. Harriman followed the report from the next sheet of paper at his place. Thirteen Curie-type power piles were now in operation, up five from the last meeting. The Susquehanna and Charleston piles had taken over the load previously borrowed from Atlantic Roadcity and the roadways of that city were now up to normal speed. It was expected that the Chicago-Angeles road could be restored to speed during the next fortnight. Power would continue to be rationed, but the crisis was over.

All very interesting but of no direct interest to Harriman. The power crisis that had been caused by the explosion of the power satellite was being satisfactorily met—very good, but Harriman's interest in it lay in the fact that the cause of interplanetary travel had thereby received a setback from which it might not recover.

When the Harper-Erickson isotopic artificial fuels had been developed three years before it had seemed that, in addition to solving the dilemma of an impossibly dangerous power source which was also utterly necessary to the economic life of the continent, an easy means had been found to achieve interplanetary travel.

The Arizona power pile had been installed in one of the largest of the Antipodes rockets, the rocket powered with isotopic fuel created in the power pile itself, and the whole thing was placed in an orbit around the Earth. A much smaller rocket had shuttled between satellite and Earth, carrying supplies to the staff of the power pile, bringing back synthetic radioactive fuel for the power-hungry technology of Earth.

As a director of the power syndicate Harriman had backed the power satellite—with a private ax to grind: he expected to power a Moon ship with fuel manufactured in the power satellite and thus to achieve the first trip to the Moon almost at once. He had not even attempted to stir the Department of Defense out of its sleep; he wanted no government subsidy—the job was a cinch; anybody could do it—and Harriman *would* do it. He had the ship; shortly he would have the fuel.

The ship had been a freighter of his own Antipodes line, her chem-fuel motors replaced, her wings removed. She still waited, ready for fuel—the recommissioned *Santa Maria*, née *City of Brisbane*.

But the fuel was slow in coming. Fuel had to be earmarked for the shuttle rocket; the power needs of a rationed continent came next—and those needs grew faster than the power satellite could turn out fuel. Far from being ready to supply him for a "useless" Moon trip, the syndicate had seized on the safe but less efficient low-temperature uranium salts and heavy water, Curie-type power piles as a means of using uranium directly to meet the ever growing need for power rather than build and launch more satellites.

Unfortunately the Curie piles did not provide the fierce star-interior conditions necessary to breeding the isotopic fuels needed for an atom-powered rocket. Harriman had reluctantly come around to the notion that he would have to use political pressure to squeeze the necessary priority for the fuels he wanted for the *Santa Maria*.

Then the power satellite had blown up.

Harriman was stirred out of his brown study by Dixon's voice. "The operations report seems satisfactory, gentlemen. If there is no objection, it will be recorded as accepted. You will note that in the next ninety days we will be back up to the power level which existed before we were forced to close down the Arizona pile."

"But with no provision for future needs," pointed out Harriman. "There have been a lot of babies born while we have been sitting here."

"Is that an objection to accepting the report, D. D.?"

"No."

"Very well. Now the public relations report—let me call attention to the first item, gentlemen. The vice-president in charge recommends a schedule of annuities, benefits, scholarships and so forth for dependents of the staff of the power satellite and of the pilot of the *Charon:* see appendix 'C.' "

A director across from Harriman—Phineas Morgan, chairman of the food trust, Cuisine, Incorporated—protested, "What is this, Ed? Too bad they were killed of course, but we paid them sky-high wages and carried their insurance to boot. Why the charity?"

Harriman grunted. "Pay it—I so move. It's peanuts. 'Do not bind the mouths of the kine who tread the grain.' "

"I wouldn't call better than nine hundred thousand 'peanuts,' " protested Morgan.

"Just a minute, gentlemen—" It was the vice-president in charge of public relations, himself a director. "If you'll look at the breakdown, Mr. Morgan, you will see that eighty-five percent of the appropriation will be used to publicize the gifts."

Morgan squinted at the figures. "Oh—why didn't you say so? Well, I suppose the gifts can be considered unavoidable overhead, but it's a bad precedent."

"Without them we have nothing to publicize."

"Yes, but—"

Dixon rapped smartly. "Mr. Harriman has moved acceptance. Please signal your desires." The tally board glowed green; even Morgan, after hesitation, okayed the allotment. "We have a related item next," said Dixon. "A Mrs.—uh, Garfield, through her attorneys, alleges that we are responsible for the congenital crippled condition of her fourth child. The putative facts are that her child was being born just as the satellite exploded and that Mrs. Garfield was then on the meridian underneath the satellite. She wants the court to award her half a million."

Morgan looked at Harriman. "Delos, I suppose that *you* will say to settle out of court."

"Don't be silly. We fight it."

Dixon looked around, surprised. "Why, D. D.? It's my guess we could settle for ten or fifteen thousand—and that was what I was about to recommend. I'm surprised that the legal department referred it to publicity."

"It's obvious why; it's loaded with high explosive. But we should fight, regardless of bad publicity. It's not like the last case; Mrs. Garfield and her brat are not our people. And any dumb fool knows you can't mark a baby by radioactivity at birth; you have to get at the germ plasm of the previous generation at least. In the third place, if we let this get by, we'll be sued for every double-yolked egg that's laid from now on. This calls for an open allotment for defense and not one damned cent for compromise."

"It might be very expensive," observed Dixon.

"It'll be more expensive not to fight. If we have to, we should buy the judge."

The public relations chief whispered to Dixon, then announced, "I support Mr. Harriman's view. That's my department's recommendation."

It was approved. "The next item," Dixon went on, "is a whole sheaf of suits arising out of slowing down the roadcities to divert power during the crisis. They allege loss of business, loss of time, loss of this and that, but they are all based on the same issue. The most touchy, perhaps, is a stockholder's suit which claims that Roadways and this company are so interlocked that the decision to divert the power was not done in the interests of the stockholders of Roadways. Delos, this is your pidgin; want to speak on it?"

"Forget it."

"Why?"

"Those are shotgun suits. This corporation is not responsible; I saw to it that Roadways volunteered to sell the power because I anticipated this. And the directorates don't interlock; not on paper, they don't. That's why dummies were born. Forget it— for every suit you've got there, Roadways has a dozen. We'll beat them."

"What makes you so sure?"

"Well—" Harriman lounged back and hung a knee over the arm of his chair. "A good many years ago I was a Western Union messenger boy. While waiting around the office I read everything I could lay hands on, including the contract on the back of the telegram forms. Remember those? They used to come in big pads of yellow paper; by writing a message on the face of the form you accepted the contract in the fine print on the back—only most people didn't realize that. Do you know what that contract obligated the company to do?"

"Send a telegram, I suppose."

"It didn't promise a darn thing. The company offered to *attempt* to deliver the message, by camel caravan or snail back, or some equally streamlined method, if convenient, but in event of failure, the company was not responsible. I read that fine print until I knew it by heart. It was the loveliest piece of prose

I had ever seen. Since then all my contracts have been worded on the same principle. Anybody who sues Roadways will find that Roadways can't be sued on the element of time, because time is not of the essence. In the event of complete nonperformance—which hasn't happened yet—Roadways is financially responsible only for freight charges or the price of the personal transportation tickets. So forget it."

Morgan sat up. "D. D., suppose I decided to run up to my country place tonight, by the roadway, and there was a failure of some sort so that I didn't get there until tomorrow? You mean to say Roadways is not liable?"

Harriman grinned. "Roadways is not liable even if you starve to death on the trip. Better use your copter." He turned back to Dixon. "I move that we stall these suits and let Roadways carry the ball for us."

"The regular agenda being completed," Dixon announced later, "time is allotted for our colleague, Mr. Harriman, to speak on a subject of his own choosing. He has not listed a subject in advance, but we will listen until it is your pleasure to adjourn."

Morgan looked sourly at Harriman. "I move we adjourn."

Harriman grinned. "For two cents I'd second that and let you die of curiosity." The motion failed for want of a second. Harriman stood up.

"Mr. Chairman, friends—" he then looked at Morgan "—and associates. As you know, I am interested in space travel."

Dixon looked at him sharply. "Not that again, Delos! If I weren't in the chair, I'd move to adjourn myself."

" 'That again,' " agreed Harriman. "Now and forever. Hear me out. Three years ago, when we were crowded into moving the Arizona power pile out into space, it looked as if we had a bonus in the shape of interplanetary travel. Some of you here joined with me in forming Spaceways, Incorporated, for experimentation, exploration—and exploitation.

"Space was conquered; rockets that could establish orbits around the globe could be modified to get to the Moon—and from there, anywhere! It was just a matter of doing it. The problems remaining were financial—and political.

"In fact, the real engineering problems of space travel have been solved since World War II. Conquering space has long been a matter of money and politics. But it did seem that the Harper-Erickson process, with its concomitant of a round-the-globe rocket and a practical economical rocket fuel, had at last made it a very present thing, so close indeed that I did not object when the early allotments of fuel from the satellite were earmarked for industrial power."

He looked around. "I shouldn't have kept quiet. I should have squawked and brought pressure and made a hairy nuisance of myself until you allotted fuel to get rid of me. For now we have missed our best chance. The satellite is gone; the source of fuel is gone. Even the shuttle rocket is gone. We are back where we were in 1950. Therefore—"

He paused again. "Therefore—I propose that we build a spaceship and send it to the Moon!"

Dixon broke the silence. "Delos, have you come unzipped? You just said that it was no longer possible. Now you say to build one."

"I didn't say it was impossible; I said we had missed our best chance. The time is overripe for space travel. This globe grows more crowded every day. In spite of technical advances the daily food intake on this planet is lower than it was thirty years ago—and we get 46 new babies every minute, 65,000 every day, 25,000,000 every year. Our race is about to burst forth to the planets; if we've got the initiative God promised an oyster we will help it along!

"Yes, we missed our best chance—but the engineering details can be solved. The real question is who's going to foot the bill? That is why I address you gentlemen, for right here in this room is the financial capital of this planet."

Morgan stood up. "Mr. Chairman, if all *company* business is finished, I ask to be excused."

Dixon nodded. Harriman said, "So long, Phineas. Don't let me keep you. Now, as I was saying, it's a money problem and here is where the money is. I move we finance a trip to the Moon."

The proposal produced no special excitement; these men knew Harriman. Presently Dixon said, "Is there a second to D. D.'s proposal?"

"Just a minute, Mr. Chairman—" It was Jack Entenza, president of Two-Continents Amusement Corporation. "I want to ask Delos some questions." He turned to Harriman. "D. D., you know I strung along when you set up Spaceways. It seemed like a cheap venture and possibly profitable in educational and scientific values—I never did fall for space liners plying between planets; that's fantastic. I don't mind playing along with your dreams to a moderate extent, but how do you propose to get to the Moon? As you say, you are fresh out of fuel."

Harriman was still grinning. "Don't kid me, Jack, I know why you came along. You weren't interested in science; you've never contributed a dime to science. You expected a monopoly on pix and television for your chain. Well, you'll get 'em, if you stick with me—otherwise I'll sign up 'Recreations, Unlimited'; they'll pay just to have you in the eye."

Entenza looked at him suspiciously. "What will it cost me?"

"Your other shirt, your eyeteeth, and your wife's wedding ring—unless 'Recreations' will pay more."

"Damn you, Delos, you're crookeder than a dog's hind leg."

"From you, Jack, that's a compliment. We'll do business. Now as to how I'm going to get to the Moon, that's a silly question. There's not a man in here who can cope with anything more complicated in the way of machinery than a knife and fork. You can't tell a left-handed monkey wrench from a reaction engine, yet you ask me for blueprints of a spaceship.

"Well, I'll tell you how I'll get to the Moon. I'll hire the proper brain boys, give them everything they want, see to it that they have all the money they can use, sweet talk them into long hours—then stand back and watch them produce. I'll run it like the Manhattan Project—most of you remember the A-bomb job; shucks, some of you can remember the Mississippi Bubble. The chap that headed up the Manhattan Project didn't know a neutron from Uncle George—but he got results. They solved that trick *four ways*. That's why I'm not worried about fuel; we'll get a fuel. We'll get several fuels."

Dixon said, "Suppose it works? Seems to me you're asking us to bankrupt the company for an exploit with no real value, aside from pure science, and a one-shot entertainment exploitation. I'm not against you—I wouldn't mind putting in ten, fifteen thousand to support a worthy venture—but I can't see the thing as a business proposition."

Harriman leaned on his fingertips and stared down the long table. "Ten or fifteen thousand gumdrops! Dan, I mean to get into you for a couple of megabucks *at least*—and before we're through you'll be hollering for more stock. This is the greatest real estate venture since the Pope carved up the New World. Don't ask me what we'll make a profit on; I can't itemize the assets—but I can lump them. The assets are a planet—a *whole planet,* Dan, that's never been touched. And more planets beyond it. If we can't figure out ways to swindle a few fast bucks out of a sweet setup like that then you and I had better both go on relief. It's like having Manhattan Island offered to you for twenty-four dollars and a case of whiskey."

Dixon grunted. "You make it sound like the chance of a lifetime."

"Chance of a lifetime, nuts! This is the greatest chance in all history. It's raining soup; grab yourself a bucket."

Next to Entenza sat Gaston P. Jones, director of Trans-America and half a dozen other banks, one of the richest men in the room. He carefully removed two inches of cigar ash, then said dryly, "Mr. Harriman, I will sell you all of my interest in the Moon, present and future, for fifty cents."

Harriman looked delighted. "Sold!"

Entenza had been pulling at his lower lip and listening with a brooding expression on his face. Now he spoke up. "Just a minute, Mr. Jones—I'll give you a dollar for it."

"Dollar fifty," answered Harriman.

"Two dollars," Entenza answered slowly.

"Five!"

They edged each other up. At ten dollars Entenza let Harriman have it and sat back, still looking thoughtful. Harriman looked happily around. "Which one of you thieves is a lawyer?" he demanded. The remark was rhetorical; out of seventeen directors the normal percentage—eleven, to be exact—were lawyers. "Hey, Tony," he continued, "draw me up an instrument right *now* that will tie down this transaction so that it couldn't be broken before the Throne of God. All of Mr. Jones' interests, rights, title, natural interest, future interests, interests held directly or through ownership of stock, presently held or to be acquired, and so forth and so forth. Put lots of Latin in it. The idea is that every interest in the Moon that Mr. Jones now has or may acquire is mine—for a ten spot, cash in hand paid." Harriman slapped a bill down on the table. "That right, Mr. Jones?"

Jones smiled briefly. "That's right, young fellow." He pocketed the bill. "I'll frame this for my grandchildren—to show them how easy it is to make money." Entenza's eyes darted from Jones to Harriman.

"Good!" said Harriman. "Gentlemen, Mr. Jones has set a market price for one human being's interest in our satellite. With around three billion persons on this globe that sets a price on the Moon of thirty billion dollars." He hauled out a wad of money. "Any more suckers? I'm buying every share that's offered, ten bucks a copy."

"I'll pay twenty!" Entenza rapped out.

Harriman looked at him sorrowfully. "Jack—don't do that! We're on the same team. Let's take the shares together, at ten."

Dixon pounded for order. "Gentlemen, please conduct such transactions after the meeting is adjourned. Is there a second to Mr. Harriman's motion?"

Gaston Jones said, "I owe it to Mr. Harriman to second his motion, without prejudice. Let's get on with a vote."

No one objected; the vote was taken. It went eleven to three against Harriman—Harriman, Strong, and Entenza for; all others against. Harriman popped up before anyone could move to adjourn and said, "I expected that. My real purpose is this: since the company is no longer interested in space travel, will it do me the courtesy of selling me what I may need of patents, processes, facilities, and so forth now held by the company but relating to space travel and not relating to the production of power on this planet? Our brief honeymoon with the power satellite built up a backlog; I want to use it. Nothing formal— just a vote that it is the policy of the company to assist me in any way not inconsistent with the primary interests of the company. How about it, gentlemen? It'll get me out of your hair."

Jones studied his cigar again. "I see no reason why we should not accommodate him, gentlemen . . . and I speak as the perfect disinterested party."

"I think we can do it, Delos," agreed Dixon, "only we won't sell you anything, we'll *lend* it to you. Then, if you happen to hit the jackpot, the company still retains an interest. Has anyone any objection?" he said to the room at large.

There was none; the matter was recorded as company policy and the meeting was adjourned. Harriman stopped to whisper with Entenza and, finally, to make an appointment. Gaston Jones stood near the door, speaking privately with Chairman Dixon. He beckoned to Strong, Harriman's partner. "George, may I ask a personal question?"

"I don't guarantee to answer. Go ahead."

"You've always struck me as a levelheaded man. Tell me—

why do you string along with Harriman? Why, the man's mad as a hatter."

Strong looked sheepish. "I ought to deny that, he's my friend . . . but I can't. But doggone it! every time Delos has a wild hunch, it turns out to be the real thing. I hate to string along— it makes me nervous—but I've learned to trust his hunches rather than another man's sworn financial report."

Jones cocked one brow. "The Midas touch, eh?"

"You could call it that."

"Well, remember what happened to King Midas—in the long run. Good day, gentlemen."

Harriman had left Entenza; Strong joined him. Dixon stood staring at them, his face very thoughtful.

2

Harriman's home had been built at the time when everyone who could was decentralizing and going underground. Above ground there was a perfect little Cape Cod cottage—the clapboards of which concealed armor plate—and most delightful, skillfully landscaped grounds; below ground there was four or five times as much floor space, immune to anything but a direct hit and possessing an independent air supply with reserves for one thousand hours. During the Crazy Years the conventional wall surrounding the grounds had been replaced by a wall which looked the same but which would stop anything short of a broaching tank—nor were the gates weak points; their gadgets were as personally loyal as a well-trained dog.

Despite its fortresslike character the house was comfortable. It was also very expensive to keep up.

Harriman did not mind the expense; Charlotte liked the house and it gave her something to do. When they were first married she had lived uncomplainingly in a cramped flat over a grocery store; if Charlotte now liked to play house in a castle, Harriman did not mind.

But he was again starting a shoestring venture; the few thousand per month of ready cash represented by the household expenses might, at some point in the game, mean the difference between success and the sheriff's bailiffs. That night at dinner, after the servants fetched the coffee and port, he took up the matter.

"My dear, I've been wondering how you would like a few months in Florida."

His wife stared at him. "Florida? Delos, is your mind wandering? Florida is unbearable at this time of the year."

"Switzerland, then. Pick your own spot. Take a real vacation, as long as you like."

"Delos, you are up to something."

Harriman sighed. Being "up to something" was the unnameable and unforgivable crime for which any American male could be indicted, tried, convicted, and sentenced in one breath. He wondered how things had gotten rigged so that the male half of the race must always behave to suit feminine rules and feminine logic, like a snotty-nosed schoolboy in front of a stern teacher.

"In a way, perhaps. We've both agreed that this house is a bit of a white elephant. I was thinking of closing it, possibly even of disposing of the land—it's worth more now than when we bought it. Then, when we get around to it, we could build something more modern and a little less like a bombproof."

Mrs. Harriman was temporarily diverted. "Well, I *have* thought it might be nice to build another place, Delos—say a little chalet tucked away in the mountains, nothing ostentatious, not more than two servants, or three. But we won't close this place until it's built, Delos—after all, one must live somewhere."

"I was not thinking of building right away," he answered cautiously.

"Why not? We're not getting any younger, Delos; if we are to enjoy the good things of life we had better not make delays. You needn't worry about it; I'll manage everything."

Harriman turned over in his mind the possibility of letting her build to keep her busy. If he earmarked the cash for her "little chalet," she would live in a hotel nearby wherever she decided to build it—and he could sell this monstrosity they were sitting in. With the nearest roadcity now less than ten miles away, the land should bring more than Charlotte's new house would cost and he would be rid of the monthly drain on his pocketbook.

"Perhaps you are right," he agreed. "But suppose you do build at once; you won't be living here; you'll be supervising every detail of the new place. I say we should unload this place; it's eating its head off in taxes, upkeep, and running expenses."

She shook her head. "Utterly out of the question, Delos. This is my home."

He ground out an almost unsmoked cigar. "I'm sorry, Charlotte, but you can't have it both ways. If you build, you can't stay here. If you stay here, we'll close these below-ground catacombs, fire about a dozen of the parasites I keep stumbling over, and live in the cottage on the surface. I'm cutting expenses."

"Discharge the servants? Delos, if you think that I will undertake to make a home for you without a proper staff, you can just—"

"Stop it." He stood up and threw his napkin down. "It doesn't take a squad of servants to make a home. When we were first married you had *no* servants—and you washed and ironed my shirts in the bargain. But we had a home then. This place is owned by that staff you speak of. Well, we're getting rid of them, all but the cook and a handyman."

She did not seem to hear him. "Delos! sit down and behave yourself. Now what's all this about cutting expenses? Are you in some sort of trouble? Are you? Answer me!"

He sat down wearily and answered, "Does a man have to be in trouble to want to cut out unnecessary expenses?"

"In your case, yes. Now what is it? Don't try to evade me."

"Now see here, Charlotte, we agreed a long time ago that I would keep business matters in the office. As for the house, we simply don't need a house this size. It isn't as if we had a passel of kids to fill up—"

"*Oh!* Blaming me for *that* again!"

"Now see here, Charlotte," he wearily began again, "I never did blame you and I'm not blaming you now. All I ever did was suggest that we both see a doctor and find out what the trouble was that we didn't have any kids. And for twenty years you've been making me pay for that one remark. But that's all over and done with now; I was simply making the point that two people don't fill up twenty-two rooms. I'll pay a reasonable price for a new house, if you want it, and give you an ample household allowance." He started to say how much, then decided not to. "Or you can close this place and live in the cottage above. It's just that we are going to quit squandering money—for a while."

She grabbed the last phrase. " 'For a while.' What's going on, Delos? What are *you* going to squander money on?" When he did not answer she went on, "Very well, if you won't tell me, I'll call George. He will tell me."

"Don't do that, Charlotte. I'm warning you. I'll—"

"You'll what!" She studied his face. "I don't need to talk to George; I can tell by looking at you. You've got the same look on your face you had when you came home and told me that you had sunk all our money in those crazy rockets."

"Charlotte, that's not fair. Skyways paid off. It's made us a mint of money."

"That's beside the point. I know why you're acting so strangely; you've got that old trip-to-the-Moon madness again. Well, I won't stand for it, do you hear? I'll stop you; I don't have to put up with it. I'm going right down in the morning and see Mr. Kamens and find out what has to be done to make you behave yourself." The cords of her neck jerked as she spoke.

He waited, gathering his temper before going on. "Charlotte, you have no real cause for complaint. No matter what happens to me, your future is taken care of."

"Do you think I want to be a widow?"

He looked thoughtfully at her. "I wonder."

"Why—why, you heartless *beast*." She stood up. "We'll say no more about it; do you mind?" She left without waiting for an answer.

His "man" was waiting for him when he got to his room. Jenkins got up hastily and started drawing Harriman's bath. "Beat it," Harriman grunted. "I can undress myself."

"You require nothing more tonight, sir?"

"Nothing. But don't go unless you feel like it. Sit down and pour yourself a drink. Ed, how long you been married?"

"Don't mind if I do." The servant helped himself. "Twenty-three years, come May, sir."

"How's it been, if you don't mind me asking?"

"Not bad. Of course there have been times——"

"I know what you mean. Ed, if you weren't working for me, what would you be doing?"

"Well, the wife and I have talked many times of opening a little restaurant, nothing pretentious, but good. A place where a gentleman could enjoy a quiet meal of good food."

"Stag, eh?"

"No, not entirely, sir—but there would be a parlor for gentlemen only. Not even waitresses; I'd tend that room myself."

"Better look around for locations, Ed. You're practically in business."

3

Strong entered their joint offices the next morning at a precise nine o'clock, as usual. He was startled to find Harriman there before him. For Harriman to fail to show up at all meant nothing; for him to beat the clerks in was significant.

Harriman was busy with a terrestrial globe and a book——the

current Nautical Almanac, Strong observed. Harriman barely
glanced up. "Morning, George. Say, who've we got a line to in
Brazil?"

"Why?"

"I need some trained seals who speak Portuguese, that's why.
And some who speak Spanish, too. Not to mention three or four
dozen scattered around in this country. I've come across something very, very interesting. Look here . . . according to these
tables the Moon only swings about twenty-eight, just short of
twenty-nine degrees north and south of the equator." He held
a pencil against the globe and spun it. "Like that. That suggest
anything?"

"No. Except that you're getting pencil marks on a sixty dollar globe."

"And you an old real estate operator! What does a man own
when he buys a parcel of land?"

"That depends on the deed. Usually mineral rights and other
subsurface rights are—"

"Never mind that. Suppose he buys the works, without split-
ting the rights; how far down does he own? How far up does he
own?"

"Well, he owns a wedge down to the center of the Earth.
That was settled in the slant-drilling and offset oil lease cases.
Theoretically he used to own the space above the land, too, out
indefinitely, but that was modified by a series of cases after the
commercial airlines came in—and a good thing for us, too, or
we would have to pay tolls every time one of our rockets took
off for Australia."

"No, no, no, George! you didn't read those cases right. Right
of passage was established—but *ownership* of the space above
the land remained unchanged. And even right of passage was
not absolute; you can build a thousand-foot tower on your own
land right where airplanes, or rockets, or whatever, have been
in the habit of passing and the ships will thereafter have to go
above it, with no kickback on you. Remember how we had to

lease the air south of Hughes Field to insure that our approach wasn't built up?"

Strong looked thoughtful. "Yes. I see your point. The ancient principle of land ownership remains undisturbed—down to the center of the Earth, up to infinity. But what of it? It's a purely theoretical matter. You're not planning to pay tolls to operate those spaceships you're always talking about, are you?" He grudged a smile at his own wit.

"Not on your tintype. Another matter entirely. George—*who owns the Moon?*"

Strong's jaw dropped, literally. "Delos, you're joking."

"I am not. I'll ask you again: if basic law says that a man owns the wedge of sky above his farm out to infinity, *who owns the Moon?* Take a look at this globe and tell me."

Strong looked. "But it can't mean anything, Delos. Earth laws wouldn't apply to the Moon."

"They apply here and that's where I am worrying about it. The Moon stays constantly over a slice of Earth bounded by latitude twenty-nine north and the same distance south; if one man owned all that belt of Earth—it's roughly the tropical zone —then he'd own the Moon, too, wouldn't he? By all the theories of real property ownership that our courts pay any attention to. And, by direct derivation, according to the sort of logic that lawyers like, the various owners of that belt of land have title—good vendable title—to the Moon somehow lodged collectively in them. The fact that the distribution of the title is a little vague wouldn't bother a lawyer; they grow fat on just such distributed titles every time a will is probated."

"It's fantastic!"

"George, when are you going to learn that 'fantastic' is a notion that doesn't bother a lawyer?"

"You're not planning to try to buy the entire tropical zone— that's what you would have to do."

"No," Harriman said slowly, "but it might not be a bad idea to buy right, title and interest in the Moon, as it may appear, from each of the sovereign countries in that belt. If I thought I could keep it quiet and not run the market up, I might try it. You can buy a thing awful cheap from a man if he thinks it's worthless and wants to sell before you regain your senses.

"But that's not the plan," he went on. "George, I want corporations—local corporations—in every one of those countries. I want the legislature of each of those countries to grant franchises to its local corporation for lunar exploration, exploitation, et cetera, and the right to claim lunar soil on behalf of the country—with fee simple, naturally, being handed on a silver platter to the patriotic corporation that thought up the idea. And I want all this done quietly, so that the bribes won't go too high. We'll own the corporations, of course, which is why I need a flock of trained seals. There is going to be one hell of a fight one of these days over who owns the Moon; I want the deck stacked so that we win no matter how the cards are dealt."

"It will be ridiculously expensive, Delos. And you don't even know that you will ever get to the Moon, much less that it will be worth anything after you get there."

"We'll get there! It'll be more expensive not to establish these claims. Anyhow it need not be very expensive; the proper use of bribe money is a homeopathic art—you use it as a catalyst. Back in the middle of the last century four men went from California to Washington with forty thousand dollars; it was all they had. A few weeks later they were broke—but Congress had awarded them a billion dollars' worth of railroad right of way. The trick is not to run up the market."

Strong shook his head. "Your title wouldn't be any good anyhow. The Moon doesn't stay in one place; it passes *over* owned land certainly—but so does a migrating goose."

"And nobody has title to a migrating bird. I get your point—but the Moon *always* stays over that one belt. If you move a boulder in your garden, do you lose title to it? Is it still real estate? Do the title laws still stand? This is like that group of real estate cases involving wandering islands in the Mississippi,

George—the land moved as the river cut new channels, *but somebody always owned it.* In this case I plan to see to it that we are the 'somebody.' "

Strong puckered his brow. "I seem to recall that some of those island-and-riparian cases were decided one way and some another."

"We'll pick the decisions that suit us. That's why lawyers' wives have mink coats. Come on, George; let's get busy."

"On what?"

"Raising the money."

"Oh." Strong looked relieved. "I thought you were planning to use *our* money."

"I am. But it won't be nearly enough. We'll use our money for the senior financing to get things moving; in the meantime we've got to work out ways to keep the money rolling in." He pressed a switch at his desk; the face of Saul Kamens, their legal chief of staff, sprang out at him. "Hey, Saul, can you slide in for a powwow?"

"Whatever it is, just tell them 'no,' " answered the attorney. "I'll fix it."

"Good. Now come on in—they're moving Hell and I've got an option on the first ten loads."

Kamens showed up in his own good time. Some minutes later Harriman had explained his notion for claiming the Moon ahead of setting foot on it. "Besides those dummy corporations," he went on, "we need an agency that can receive contributions without having to admit any financial interest on the part of the contributor—like the National Geographic Society."

Kamens shook his head. "You can't buy the National Geographic Society."

"Damn it, who said we were going to? We'll set up our own."

"That's what I started to say."

"Good. As I see it, we need at least one tax-free, nonprofit corporation headed up by the right people—we'll hang on to voting control, of course. We'll probably need more than one;

we'll set them up as we need them. And we've got to have at least one new ordinary corporation, *not* tax free—but it won't show a profit until we are ready. The idea is to let the nonprofit corporations have all of the prestige and all of the publicity—and the other gets all of the profits, if and when. We swap assets around between corporations, always for perfectly valid reasons, so that the nonprofit corporations pay the expenses as we go along. Come to think about it, we had better have at least two ordinary corporations, so that we can let one of them go through bankruptcy if we find it necessary to shake out the water. That's the general sketch. Get busy and fix it up so that it's legal, will you?"

Kamens said, "You know, Delos, it would be a lot more honest if you did it at the point of a gun."

"A lawyer talks to me of honesty! Never mind, Saul; I'm not actually going to cheat anyone—"

"Hmmph!"

"—and I'm just going to make a trip to the Moon. That's what everybody will be paying for; that's what they'll get. Now fix it up so that it's legal, that's a good boy."

"I'm reminded of something the elder Vanderbilt's lawyer said to the old man under similar circumstances: 'It's beautiful the way it is; why spoil it by making it legal?' Okay, brother gonoph, I'll rig your trap. Anything else?"

"Sure. Stick around, you might have some ideas. George, ask Montgomery to come in, will you?" Montgomery, Harriman's publicity chief, had two virtues in his employer's eyes: he was personally loyal to Harriman, and, secondly, he was quite capable of planning a campaign to convince the public that Lady Godiva wore a Caresse-brand girdle during her famous ride . . . or that Hercules attributed his strength to Crunchies for breakfast.

He arrived with a large portfolio under his arm. "Glad you sent for me, Chief. Get a load of this—" He spread the folder open on Harriman's desk and began displaying sketches and layouts. "Kinsky's work—is that boy hot!"

Harriman closed the portfolio. "What outfit is it for?"

"Huh? New World Homes."

"I don't want to see it; we're dumping New World Homes. Wait a minute—don't start to bawl. Have the boys go through with it; I want the price kept up while we unload. But open your ears to another matter." He rapidly explained the new enterprise.

Presently Montgomery was nodding. "When do we start and how much do we spend?"

"Right away and spend what you need to. Don't get chicken about expenses; this is the biggest thing we've ever tackled." Strong flinched; Harriman went on, "Have insomnia over it tonight; see me tomorrow and we'll kick it around."

"Wait a sec, Chief. How are you going to sew up all those franchises from the, uh—the Moon states, those countries the Moon passes over, while a big publicity campaign is going on about a trip to the Moon and how big a thing it is for everybody? Aren't you about to paint yourself into a corner?"

"Do I look stupid? We'll get the franchises *before* you hand out so much as a filler—*you'll* get 'em, you and Kamens. That's your first job."

"Hmmm. . . ." Montgomery chewed a thumbnail. "Well, all right—I can see some angles. How soon do we have to sew it up?"

"I give you six weeks. Otherwise just mail your resignation in, written on the skin off your back."

"I'll write it right now, if you'll help me by holding a mirror."

"Damn it, Monty, I know you can't do it in six weeks. But make it fast; we can't take a cent in to keep the thing going until you sew up those franchises. If you dillydally, we'll all starve—and we won't get to the Moon, either."

Strong said, "D. D., why fiddle with these trick claims from a bunch of moth-eaten tropical countries? If you are dead set on going to the Moon, let's call Ferguson in and get on with the matter."

"I like your direct approach, George," Harriman said, frowning. "Mmmm . . . back about 1845 or '46 an eager-beaver American army officer captured California. You know what the State Department did?"

"No."

"They made him hand it back. Seems he hadn't touched second base, or something. So they had to go to the trouble of capturing it all over again a few months later. Now I don't want that to happen to us. It's not enough just to set foot on the Moon and claim it; we've got to validate that claim in terrestrial courts—or we're in for a peck of trouble. Eh, Saul?"

Kamens nodded. "Remember what happened to Columbus."

"Exactly. We aren't going to let ourselves be rooked the way Columbus was."

Montgomery spat out some thumbnail. "But, Chief—you know damn well those banana-state claims won't be worth two cents after I do tie them up. Why not get a franchise right from the UN and settle the matter? I'd as lief tackle that as tackle two dozen cockeyed legislatures. In fact I've got an angle already—we work it through the Security Council and—"

"Keep working on that angle; we'll use it later. You don't appreciate the full mechanics of the scheme, Monty. Of course those claims are worth nothing—except nuisance value. But their nuisance value is all-important. Listen: we get to the Moon, or appear about to. Every one of those countries puts up a squawk; we goose them into it through the dummy corporations they have enfranchised. Where do they squawk? To the UN, of course. Now the big countries on this globe, the rich and important ones, are all in the northern temperate zone. They see what the claims are based on and they take a frenzied look at the globe. Sure enough, the Moon does not pass over a one of them. The biggest country of all—Russia—doesn't own a spadeful of dirt south of twenty-nine north. So they reject all the claims.

"Or do they?" Harriman went on. "The U. S. balks. *The Moon passes over Florida and the southern part of Texas.* Washington is in a tizzy. Should they back up the tropical countries and support the traditional theory of land title or should they throw their weight to the idea that the Moon belongs to everyone? Or should the United States try to claim the whole thing, seeing as how it was Americans who actually got there first?

"At this point we creep out from under cover. It seems that the Moon ship was owned and the expenses paid by a nonprofit corporation chartered by the UN itself—"

"Hold it," interrupted Strong. "I didn't know that the UN could create corporations?"

"You'll find it can," his partner answered. "How about it, Saul?" Kamens nodded. "Anyway," Harriman continued, "I've already got the corporation. I had it set up several years ago. It can do most anything of an educational or scientific nature —and, brother, that covers a lot of ground! Back to the point— this corporation, this creature of the UN, asks its parent to declare the lunar colony autonomous territory, under the protection of the UN. We won't ask for outright membership at first because we want to keep it simple—"

"Simple, he calls it!" said Montgomery.

"Simple. This new colony will be a de facto sovereign state, holding title to the entire Moon, and—listen closely!—capable of buying, selling, passing laws, issuing title to land, setting up monopolies, collecting tariffs, et cetera without end. *And we own it!*

"The reason we get all this is because the major states in the UN can't think up a claim that sounds as legal as the claim made by the tropical states, they can't agree among themselves as to how to split up the swag if they were to attempt brute force and the other major states aren't willing to see the United

States claim the whole thing. They'll take the easy way out of their dilemma by appearing to retain title in the UN itself. The real title, the title controlling all economic and legal matters, will revert to us. Now do you see my point, Monty?"

Montgomery grinned. "Damned if I know if it's necessary, Chief, but I love it. It's beautiful."

"Well, I don't think so," Strong grumbled. "Delos, I've seen you rig some complicated deals—some of them so devious that they turned even my stomach—but this one is the worst yet. I think you've been carried away by the pleasure you get out of cooking up involved deals in which somebody gets double crossed."

Harriman puffed hard on his cigar before answering. "I don't give a damn, George. Call it chicanery, call it anything you want to. *I'm going to the Moon!* If I have to manipulate a million people to accomplish it, I'll do it."

"But it's not necessary to do it this way."

"Well, how would you do it?"

"Me? I'd set up a straightforward corporation. I'd get a resolution in Congress making my corporation the chosen instrument of the United States—"

"Bribery?"

"Not necessarily. Influence and pressure ought to be enough. Then I would set about raising the money and make the trip."

"And the United States would then own the Moon?"

"Naturally," Strong answered a little stiffly.

Harriman got up and began pacing. "You don't see it, George, you don't see it. The Moon was not meant to be owned by a single country, even the United States."

"It was meant to be owned by *you*, I suppose."

"Well, if I own it—for a short while—I won't misuse it and I'll take care that others don't. Damnation, nationalism should stop at the stratosphere. Can you see what would happen if the United States lays claim to the Moon? The other nations won't recognize the claim. It will become a permanent bone of contention in the Security Council—just when we were beginning to get straightened out to the point where a man could do business planning without having his elbow jogged by a war every few years. The other nations—quite rightfully—will be scared to death of the United States. They will be able to look up in the sky any night and see the main atom-bomb rocket base of the United States staring down the backs of their necks. Are they going to hold still for it? No, sirree—they are going to try to clip off a piece of the Moon for their own national use. The Moon is too big to hold, all at once. There will be other bases established there and presently there will be the Goddamnedest war this planet has ever seen—and we'll be to blame.

"No, it's got to be an arrangement that everybody will hold still for—and that's why we've got to plan it, think of all the angles, and be devious about it until we are in a position to make it work.

"Anyhow, George, if we claim it in the name of the United States, do you know where we will be, as businessmen?"

"In the driver's seat," answered Strong.

"In a pig's eye! We'll be dealt right out of the game. The Department of National Defense will say, 'Thank you, Mr. Harriman. Thank you, Mr. Strong. We are taking over in the interests of national security; you can go home now.' And that's just what we would have to do—go home and wait for the next atom war.

"I'm not going to do it, George. I'm not going to let the brass hats muscle in. I'm going to set up a lunar colony and then nurse it along until it is big enough to stand on its own feet. I'm telling you—all of you!—this is the biggest thing for the human race since the discovery of fire. Handled right, it can mean a new and braver world. Handle it wrong and it's a one-way ticket to Armageddon. It's coming, it's coming soon, whether we touch it or not. But I plan to be the Man in the Moon myself—and give it my personal attention to see that it's handled right."

He paused. Strong said, "Through with your sermon, Delos?"

"No, I'm not," Harriman denied testily. "You don't see this thing the right way. Do you know what we may find up there?" He swung his arm in an arc toward the ceiling. *"People!"*

"On the *Moon?*" said Kamens.

"Why not on the Moon?" whispered Montgomery to Strong.

"No, not on the Moon—at least I'd be amazed if we dug down and found anybody under that airless shell. The Moon has had its day; I was speaking of the other planets—Mars and Venus and the satellites of Jupiter. Even maybe out at the stars themselves. Suppose we do find people? Think what it will mean to us. We've been alone, all alone, the only intelligent race in the only world we know. We haven't even been able to talk with dogs or apes. Any answers we got we had to think up by ourselves, like deserted orphans. But suppose we find *people,* intelligent people, who have done some thinking in their own way. *We wouldn't be alone any more!* We could look up at the stars and never be afraid again."

He finished, seeming a little tired and even a little ashamed of his outburst, like a man surprised in a private act. He stood facing them, searching their faces.

"Gee whiz, Chief," said Montgomery, "I can use that. How about it?"

"Think you can remember it?"

"Don't need to—I flipped on your 'silent steno.' "

"Well, damn your eyes!"

"We'll put it on video—in a play, I think."

Harriman smiled almost boyishly. "I've never acted, but if you think it'll do any good, I'm game."

"Oh, no, not you, Chief," Montgomery answered in horrified tones. "You're not the type. I'll use Basil Wilkes-Booth, I think. With his organlike voice and that beautiful archangel face, he'll really send 'em."

Harriman glanced down at his paunch and said gruffly,

"Okay—back to business. Now about money. In the first place we can go after straight donations to one of the nonprofit corporations, just like endowments for colleges. Hit the upper brackets, where tax deductions really matter. How much do you think we can raise that way?"

"Very little," Strong opined. "That cow is about milked dry."

"It's never milked dry, as long as there are rich men around who would rather make gifts than pay taxes. How much will a man pay to have a crater on the Moon named after him?"

"I thought they all had names?" remarked the lawyer.

"Lots of them don't—and we have the whole back face that's not touched yet. We won't try to put down an estimate today; we'll just list it. Monty, I want an angle to squeeze dimes out of the school kids, too. Forty million school kids at a dime a head is four million dollars—we can use that."

"Why stop at a dime?" asked Monty. "If you get a kid really interested he'll scrape together a dollar."

"Yes, but what do we offer him for it? Aside from the honor of taking part in a noble venture and so forth?"

"Mmmm. . . ." Montgomery used up more thumbnail. "Suppose we go after both the dimes and the dollars. For a dime he gets a card saying that he's a member of the Moonbeam club—"

"No, the 'Junior Spacemen.' "

"Okay, the Moonbeams will be girls—and don't forget to rope the Boy Scouts and the Girl Scouts into it, too. We give each kid a card; when he kicks in another dime, we punch it. When he's punched out a dollar, we give him a certificate, suitable for framing, with his name and some process engraving, and on the back a picture of the Moon."

"On the *front*," answered Harriman. "Do it in one print job; it's cheaper and it'll look better. We give him something else, too, a steel-clad guarantee that his name will be on the rolls of the Junior Pioneers of the Moon, which same will be placed in a monument to be erected on the Moon at the landing site of the first Moon ship—in microfilm, of course; we have to watch weight."

"Fine!" agreed Montgomery. "Want to swap jobs, Chief? When he gets up to ten dollars we give him a genuine, solid gold-plated shooting star pin and he's a senior Pioneer, with the right to vote or something or other. And his name goes *outside* of the monument—microengraved on a platinum strip."

Strong looked as if he had bitten a lemon. "What happens when he reaches a hundred dollars?" he asked.

"Why, then," Montgomery answered happily, "we give him another card and he can start over. Don't worry about it, Mr. Strong—if any kid goes that high, he'll have his reward. Probably we will take him on an inspection tour of the ship before it takes off and give him, absolutely free, a picture of himself standing in front of it, with the pilot's own signature signed across the bottom by some female clerk."

"Chiseling from kids. Bah!"

"Not at all," answered Montgomery in hurt tones. "Intangibles are the most honest merchandise anyone can sell. They are always worth whatever you are willing to pay for them and they never wear out. You can take them to your grave untarnished."

"Hmmmph!"

Harriman listened to this, smiling and saying nothing. Kamens cleared his throat. "If you two ghouls are through cannibalizing the youth of the land, I've another idea."

"Spill it."

"George, you collect stamps, don't you?"

"Yes."

"How much would a cover be worth which had been to the Moon and been cancelled there?"

"Huh? But you couldn't, you know."

"I think we could get our Moon ship declared a legal post

office substation without too much trouble. What would it be worth?"

"Uh, that depends on how rare they are."

"There must be some optimum number which will fetch a maximum return. Can you estimate it?"

Strong got a faraway look in his eye, then took out an old-fashioned pencil and commenced to figure.

Harriman went on. "Saul, my minor success in buying a share in the Moon from Jones went to my head. How about selling building lots on the Moon?"

"Let's keep this serious, Delos. You can't do that until you've landed there."

"I am serious. I know you are thinking of that ruling back in the forties that such land would have to be staked out and accurately described. I want to sell land on the Moon. You figure out a way to make it legal. I'll sell the whole Moon, if I can—surface rights, mineral rights, anything."

"Suppose they want to occupy it?"

"Fine. The more the merrier. I'd like to point out, too, that we'll be in a position to assess taxes on what we have sold. If they don't use it and won't pay taxes, it reverts to us. Now you figure out how to offer it, without going to jail. You may have to advertise it abroad, then plan to peddle it personally in this country, like Irish Sweepstakes tickets."

Kamens looked thoughtful. "We could incorporate the land company in Panama and advertise by video and radio from Mexico. Do you really think you can sell the stuff?"

"You can sell snowballs in Greenland," put in Montgomery. "It's a matter of promotion."

Harriman added, "Did you ever read about the Florida land boom, Saul? People bought lots they had never seen and sold them at tripled prices without ever having laid eyes on them. Sometimes a parcel would change hands a dozen times before anyone got around to finding out that the stuff was ten-foot deep in water. We can offer bargains better than that—an acre, a guaranteed dry acre with plenty of sunshine, for maybe ten dollars—or a thousand acres at a dollar an acre. Who's going to turn down a bargain like that? Particularly after the rumor gets around that the Moon is believed to be loaded with uranium?"

"Is it?"

"How should I know? When the boom sags a little we will announce the selected location of Luna City—and it will just happen to work out that the land around the site is still available for sale. Don't worry, Saul, if it's real estate, George and I can sell it. Why, down in the Ozarks, where the land stands on edge, we used to sell both sides of the same acre." Harriman looked thoughtful. "I think we'll reserve mineral rights—there just might actually be uranium there!"

Kamens chuckled. "Delos, you are a kid at heart. Just a great big, overgrown, lovable—juvenile delinquent."

Strong straightened up. "I make it half a million," he said.

"Half a million what?" asked Harriman.

"For the cancelled philatelic covers, of course. That's what we were talking about. Five thousand is my best estimate of the number that could be placed with serious collectors and with dealers. Even then we will have to discount them to a syndicate and hold back until the ship is built and the trip looks like a probability."

"Okay," agreed Harriman. "You handle it. I'll just note that we can tap you for an extra half million toward the end."

"Don't I get a commission?" asked Kamens. "I thought of it."

"You get a rising vote of thanks—and ten acres on the Moon. Now what other sources of revenue can we hit?"

"Don't you plan to sell stocks?" asked Kamens.

"I was coming to that. Of course—but no preferred stock; we don't want to be forced through a reorganization. Participating common, nonvoting—"

"Sounds like another banana-state corporation to me."

"Naturally—but I want some of it on the New York Exchange, and you'll have to work that out with the Securities Exchange Commission somehow. Not too much of it—that's our showcase and we'll have to keep it active and moving up."

"Wouldn't you rather I swam the Hellespont?"

"Don't be like that, Saul. It beats chasing ambulances, doesn't it?"

"I'm not sure."

"Well, that's what I want you—wups!" The screen on Harriman's desk had come to life. A girl said, "Mr. Harriman, Mr. Dixon is here. He has no appointment but he says that you want to see him."

"I thought I had that thing shut off," muttered Harriman, then pressed his key and said, "Okay, show him in."

"Very well, sir—oh, Mr. Harriman, Mr. Entenza came in just this second."

"Send them both in." Harriman disconnected and turned back to his associates. "Zip your lips, gang, and hold on to your wallets."

"Look who's talking," said Kamens.

Dixon came in with Entenza behind him. He sat down, looked around, started to speak, then checked himself. He looked around again, especially at Entenza.

"Go ahead, Dan," Harriman encouraged him. "'Tain't nobody here at all but just us chickens."

Dixon made up his mind. "I've decided to come in with you, D. D.," he announced. "As an act of faith I went to the trouble of getting this." He took a formal-looking instrument from his pocket and displayed it. It was a sale of lunar rights, from Phineas Morgan to Dixon, phrased in exactly the same fashion as that which Jones had granted to Harriman.

Entenza looked startled, then dipped into his own inner coat pocket. Out came three more sales contracts of the same sort,

each from a director of the power syndicate. Harriman cocked
an eyebrow at them. "Jack sees you and raises you two, Dan.
You want to call?"

Dixon smiled ruefully. "I can just see him." He added two
more to the pile, grinned and offered his hand to Entenza.

"Looks like a standoff." Harriman decided to say nothing
just yet about seven telestated contracts now locked in his desk
—after going to bed the night before he had been quite busy on
the phone almost till midnight. "Jack, how much did you pay
for those things?"

"Standish held out for a thousand; the others were cheap."

"Damn it, I warned you not to run the price up. Standish will
gossip. How about you, Dan?"

"I got them at satisfactory prices."

"So you won't talk, eh? Never mind—gentlemen, how serious are you about this? How much money did you bring?"

Entenza looked to Dixon, who answered, "How much does
it take?"

"How much can you raise?" demanded Harriman.

Dixon shrugged. "We're getting no place. Let's use figures.
A hundred thousand."

Harriman sniffed. "I take it what you really want is to reserve
a seat on the first regularly scheduled Moon ship. I'll sell it to
you at that price."

"Let's quit sparring, Delos. How much?"

Harriman's face remained calm but he thought furiously. He
was caught short, with too little information—he had not even
talked figures with his chief engineer as yet. Confound it! why
had he left that phone hooked in? "Dan, as I warned you, it will
cost you at least a million just to sit down in this game."

"So I thought. How much will it take to *stay* in the game?"

"All you've got."

"Don't be silly, Delos. I've got more than you have."

Harriman lit a cigar, his only sign of agitation. "Suppose you
match us, dollar for dollar."

"For which I get two shares?"

"Okay, okay, you chuck in a buck whenever each of us does —share and share alike. But I run things."

"You run the operations," agreed Dixon. "Very well, I'll put up a million now and match you as necessary. You have no objection to me having my own auditor, of course."

"When have I ever cheated you, Dan?"

"Never and there is no need to start."

"Have it your own way—but be damned sure you send a man who can keep his mouth shut."

"He'll keep quiet. I keep his heart in a jar in my safe."

Harriman was thinking about the extent of Dixon's assets. "We just might let you buy in with a second share later, Dan. This operation will be expensive."

Dixon fitted his fingertips carefully together. "We'll meet that question when we come to it. I don't believe in letting an enterprise fold up for lack of capital."

"Good." Harriman turned to Entenza. "You heard what Dan had to say, Jack. Do you like the terms?"

Entenza's forehead was covered with sweat. "I can't raise a million that fast."

"That's all right, Jack. We don't need it this morning. Your note is good; you can take your time liquidating."

"But you said a million is just the beginning. I can't match you indefinitely; you've got to place a limit on it. I've got my family to consider."

"No annuities, Jack? No monies transferred in an irrevocable trust?"

"That's not the point. You'll be able to squeeze me—freeze me out."

Harriman waited for Dixon to say something. Dixon finally said, "We wouldn't squeeze you, Jack—as long as you could prove you had converted every asset you hold. We would let you stay in on a pro rata basis."

Harriman nodded. "That's right, Jack." He was thinking that

any shrinkage in Entenza's share would give himself and Strong a clear voting majority.

Strong had been thinking of something of the same nature, for he spoke up suddenly, "I don't like this. Four equal partners —we can be deadlocked too easily."

Dixon shrugged. "I refuse to worry about it. I am in this because I am betting that Delos can manage to make it profitable."

"We'll get to the Moon, Dan!"

"I didn't say that. I am betting that you will show a profit whether we get to the Moon or not. Yesterday evening I spent looking over the public records of several of your companies; they were very interesting. I suggest we resolve any possible deadlock by giving the Director—that's you, Delos—the power to settle ties. Satisfactory, Entenza?"

"Oh, sure!"

Harriman was worried but tried not to show it. He did not trust Dixon, even bearing gifts. He stood up suddenly. "I've got to run, gentlemen. I leave you to Mr. Strong and Mr. Kamens. Come along, Monty." Kamens, he was sure, would not spill anything prematurely, even to nominal full partners. As for Strong—George, he knew, had not even let his left hand know how many fingers there were on his right.

He dismissed Montgomery outside the door of the partners' personal office and went across the hall. Andrew Ferguson, chief engineer of Harriman Enterprises, looked up as he came in. "Howdy, Boss. Say, Mr. Strong gave me an interesting idea for a light switch this morning. It did not seem practical at first but—"

"Skip it. Let one of the boys have it and forget it. You know the line we are on now."

"There have been rumors," Ferguson answered cautiously.

"Fire the man that brought you the rumor. No—send him on a special mission to Tibet and keep him there until we are through. Well, let's get on with it. I want you to build a Moon ship as quickly as possible."

Ferguson threw one leg over the arm of his chair, took out a penknife and began grooming his nails. "You say that like it was an order to build a privy."

"Why not? There have been theoretically adequate fuels since way back in '49. You get together the team to design it and the gang to build it; you build it—I pay the bills. What could be simpler?"

Ferguson stared at the ceiling. " 'Adequate fuels—' " he repeated dreamily.

"So I said. The figures show that hydrogen and oxygen are enough to get a step rocket to the Moon and back—it's just a matter of proper design."

" 'Proper design,' he says," Ferguson went on in the same gentle voice, then suddenly swung around, jabbed the knife into the scarred desk top and bellowed, "What do you know about proper design? Where do I get the steels? What do I use for a throat liner? How in the hell do I burn enough tons of your crazy mix per second to keep from wasting all my power breaking loose? How can I get a decent mass ratio with a step rocket? Why in the hell didn't you let me build a proper ship when we had the fuel?"

Harriman waited for him to quiet down, then said, "What do we do about it, Andy?"

"Hmmm. . . . I was thinking about it as I lay abed last night—and my old lady is sore as hell at you; I had to finish the night on the couch. In the first place, Mr. Harriman, the proper way to tackle this is to get a research appropriation from the Department of National Defense. Then you—"

"Damn it, Andy, you stick to engineering and let me handle the political and financial end of it. I don't want your advice."

"Damn it, Delos, don't go off half cocked. This *is* engineering I'm talking about. The government owns a whole mass of for-

mer art about rocketry—all classified. Without a government
contract you can't even get a peek at it."

"It can't amount to very much. What can a government
rocket do that a Skyways rocket can't do? You told me yourself that Federal rocketry no longer amounted to anything."

Ferguson looked supercilious. "I am afraid I can't explain it
in lay terms. You will have to take it for granted that we need
those government research reports. There's no sense in spending
thousands of dollars in doing work that has already been done."

"Spend the thousands."

"Maybe millions."

"Spend the millions. Don't be afraid to spend money. Andy,
I don't want this to be a military job." He considered elabo-
rating to the engineer the involved politics back of his decision,
thought better of it. "How bad do you actually need that government stuff? Can't you get the same results by hiring engineers who used to work for the government? Or even hire them
away from the government right now?"

Ferguson pursed his lips. "If you insist on hampering me,
how can you expect me to get results?"

"I am not hampering you. I am telling you that this is not a
government project. If you won't attempt to cope with it on
those terms, let me know now, so that I can find somebody who
will."

Ferguson started playing mumblety-peg on his desk top.
When he got to "noses"—and missed—he said quietly, "I mind
a boy who used to work for the government at White Sands. He
was a very smart lad indeed—design chief of section."

"You mean he might head up your team?"

"That was the notion."

"What's his name? Where is he? Who's he working for?"

"Well, as it happened, when the government closed down
White Sands, it seemed a shame to me that a good boy should
be out of a job, so I placed him with Skyways. He's maintenance chief engineer out on the Coast."

"Maintenance? What a hell of a job for a creative man! But you mean he's working for us now? Get him on the screen. No —call the Coast and have them send him here in a special rocket; we'll all have lunch together."

"As it happens," Ferguson said quietly, "I got up last night and called him—that's what annoyed the Missus. He's waiting outside. Coster—Bob Coster."

A slow grin spread over Harriman's face. "Andy! You black-hearted old scoundrel, why did you pretend to balk?"

"I wasn't pretending. I like it here, Mr. Harriman. Just as long as you don't interfere, I'll do my job. Now my notion is this: we'll make young Coster chief engineer of the project and give him his head. I won't joggle his elbow; I'll just read the reports. Then you leave him alone, d'you hear me? Nothing makes a good technical man angrier than to have some incompetent nitwit with a checkbook telling him how to do his job."

"Suits. And I don't want a penny-pinching old fool slowing him down, either. Mind you don't interfere with him, either, or I'll jerk the rug out from under you. Do we understand each other?"

"I think we do."

"Then get him in here."

Apparently Ferguson's concept of a "lad" was about age thirty-five, for such Harriman judged Coster to be. He was tall, lean, and quietly eager. Harriman braced him immediately, after shaking hands with, "Bob, can you build a rocket that will go to the Moon?"

Coster took it without blinking. "Do you have a source of X-fuel?" he countered, giving the rocket man's usual shorthand for the isotope fuel formerly produced by the power satellite.

"No."

Coster remained perfectly quiet for several seconds, then answered, "I can put an unmanned messenger rocket on the face of the Moon."

"Not good enough. I want it to go there, land, and come

back. Whether it lands here under power or by atmosphere braking is unimportant."

It appeared that Coster never answered promptly; Harriman had the fancy that he could hear wheels turning over in the man's head. "That would be a very expensive job."

"Who asked you how much it would cost? Can you do it?"

"I could try."

"Try, hell. Do you think you can do it? Would you bet your shirt on it? Would you be willing to risk your neck in the attempt? If you don't believe in yourself, man, you'll always lose."

"How much will *you* risk, sir? I told you this would be expensive—and I doubt if you have any idea how expensive."

"And I told you not to worry about money. Spend what you need; it's my job to pay the bills. Can you do it?"

"I can do it. I'll let you know later how much it will cost and how long it will take."

"Good. Start getting your team together. Where are we going to do this, Andy?" he added, turning to Ferguson. "Australia?"

"No." It was Coster who answered. "It can't be Australia; I want a mountain catapult. That will save us one step-combination."

"How big a mountain?" asked Harriman. "Will Pikes Peak do?"

"It ought to be in the Andes," objected Ferguson. "The mountains are taller and closer to the equator. After all, we own facilities there—or the Andes Development Company does."

"Do as you like, Bob," Harriman told Coster. "I would prefer Pikes Peak, but it's up to you." He was thinking that there were tremendous business advantages to locating Earth's spaceport number 1 inside the United States—and he could visualize the advertising advantage of having Moon ships blast off from the top of Pikes Peak, in plain view of everyone for hundreds of miles to the East.

"I'll let you know."

"Now about salary. Forget whatever it was we were paying you; how much do you want?"

Coster actually gestured, waving the subject away. "I'll work for coffee and cakes."

"Don't be silly."

"Let me finish. Coffee and cakes and one other thing: I get to make the trip."

Harriman blinked. "Well, I can understand that," he said slowly. "In the meantime I'll put you on a drawing account." He added, "Better calculate for a three-man ship, unless you are a pilot."

"I'm not."

"Three men, then. You see, I'm going along, too."

4

"A good thing you decided to come in, Dan," Harriman was saying, "or you would find yourself out of a job. I'm going to put an awful crimp in the power company before I'm through with this."

Dixon buttered a roll. "Really? How?"

"We'll set up high-temperature piles, like the Arizona job, just like the one that blew up, around the corner on the far face of the Moon. We'll remote-control them; if one explodes it won't matter. And I'll breed more X-fuel in a week than the company turned out in three months. Nothing personal about it; it's just that I want a source of fuel for interplanetary liners. If we can't get good stuff here, we'll have to make it on the Moon."

"Interesting. But where do you propose to get the uranium for six piles? The last I heard the Atomic Energy Commission had the prospective supply earmarked twenty years ahead."

"Uranium? Don't be silly; we'll get it on the Moon."

"On the Moon? Is there uranium on the Moon?"

"Didn't you know? I thought that was why you decided to join up with me."

"No, I didn't know," Dixon said deliberately. "What proof have you?"

"Me? I'm no scientist, but it's a well-understood fact. Spectroscopy, or something. Catch one of the professors. But don't go showing too much interest; we aren't ready to show our hand." Harriman stood up. "I've got to run, or I'll miss the shuttle for Rotterdam. Thanks for the lunch." He grabbed his hat and left.

Harriman stood up. "Suit yourself, Mynheer van der Velde. I'm giving you and your colleagues a chance to hedge your bets. Your geologists all agree that diamonds result from volcanic action. What do you think we will find *there?*" He dropped a large photograph of the Moon on the Hollander's desk.

The diamond merchant looked impassively at the pictured planet, pockmarked by a thousand giant craters. "If you get there, Mr. Harriman."

Harriman swept up the picture. "We'll get there. And we'll find diamonds—though I would be the first to admit that it may be twenty years or even forty before there is a big enough strike to matter. I've come to you because I believe that the worst villain in our social body is the man who introduces a major new economic factor without planning his innovation in such a way as to permit peaceful adjustment. I don't like panics. But all I can do is warn you. Good day."

"Sit down, Mr. Harriman. I'm always confused when a man explains how he is going to do *me* good. Suppose you tell me instead how this is going to do *you* good? Then we can discuss how to protect the world market against a sudden influx of diamonds from the Moon."

Harriman sat down.

Harriman liked the Low Countries. He was delighted to lo-

cate a dog-drawn milk cart whose young master wore real
wooden shoes; he happily took pictures and tipped the child
heavily, unaware that the setup was arranged for tourists. He
visited several other diamond merchants but without speaking
of the Moon. Among other purchases he found a brooch for
Charlotte—a peace offering.

Then he took a taxi to London, planted a story with the representatives of the diamond syndicate there, arranged with his
London solicitors to be insured by Lloyd's of London, through
a dummy, *against* a successful Moon flight, and called his home
office. He listened to numerous reports, especially those con-
cerning Montgomery, and found that Montgomery was in New
Delhi. He called him there, spoke with him at length, then hurried to the port just in time to catch his ship. He was in Colorado the next morning.

At Peterson Field, east of Colorado Springs, he had trouble
getting through the gate, even though it was now his domain,
under lease. Of course he could have called Coster and gotten
it straightened out at once, but he wanted to look around before
seeing Coster. Fortunately the head guard knew him by sight;
he got in and wandered around for an hour or more, a tri-col-
ored badge pinned to his coat to give him freedom.

The machine shop was moderately busy, so was the foundry
. . . but most of the shops were almost deserted. Harriman left
the shops, went into the main engineering building. The drafting room and the loft were fairly active, as was the computation section. But there were unoccupied desks in the structures
group and a churchlike quiet in the metals group and in the ad-
joining metallurgical laboratory. He was about to cross over
into the chemicals and materials annex when Coster suddenly
showed up.

"Mr. Harriman! I just heard you were here."

"Spies everywhere," remarked Harriman. "I didn't want to
disturb you."

"Not at all. Let's go up to my office."

Settled there a few moments later, Harriman asked, "Well—how's it going?"

Coster frowned. "All right, I guess."

Harriman noted that the engineer's desk baskets were piled high with papers which spilled over onto the desk. Before Harriman could answer, Coster's desk phone lit up and a feminine voice said sweetly, "Mr. Coster—Mr. Morgenstern is calling."

"Tell him I'm busy."

After a short wait the girl answered in a troubled voice, "He says he's just got to speak to you, sir."

Coster looked annoyed. "Excuse me a moment, Mr. Harriman—Okay, put him on."

The girl was replaced by a man who said, "Oh, there you are —what was the holdup? Look, Chief, we're in a jam about these trucks. Every one of them that we leased needs an overhaul and now it turns out that the White Fleet company won't do anything about it—they're sticking to the fine print in the contract. Now the way I see it, we'd do better to cancel the contract and do business with Peak City Transport. They have a scheme that looks good to me. They guarantee to—"

"Take care of it," snapped Coster. "You made the contract and you have authority to cancel. You know that."

"Yes, but Chief, I figured this would be something you would want to pass on personally. It involves policy and—"

"Take care of it! I don't give a damn what you do as long as we have transportation when we need it." He switched off.

"Who is that man?" inquired Harriman.

"Who? Oh, that's Morgenstern, Claude Morgenstern."

"Not his name—what does he do?"

"He's one of my assistants—buildings, grounds, and transportation."

"Fire him!"

Coster looked stubborn. Before he could answer, a secretary came in and stood insistently at his elbow with a sheaf of papers. He frowned, initialed them, and sent her out.

"Oh, I don't mean that as an order," Harriman added, "but I do mean it as serious advice. I won't give orders in your backyard, but will you listen to a few minutes of advice?"

"Naturally," Coster agreed stiffly.

"Mmm . . . this your first job as top boss?"

Coster hesitated, then admitted it.

"I hired you on Ferguson's belief that you were the engineer most likely to build a successful Moon ship. I've had no reason to change my mind. But top administration ain't engineering, and maybe I can show you a few tricks there, if you'll let me." He waited. "I'm not criticizing," he added. "Top bossing is like sex; until you've had it, you don't know about it." Harriman had the mental reservation that if the boy would not take advice, he would suddenly be out of a job, whether Ferguson liked it or not.

Coster drummed on his desk. "I don't know what's wrong and that's a fact. It seems as if I can't turn anything over to anybody and have it done properly. I feel as if I were swimming in quicksand."

"Done much engineering lately?"

"I try to." Coster waved at another desk in the corner. "I work there, late at night."

"That's no good. I hired you as an engineer. Bob, this setup is all wrong. The joint ought to be jumping—and it's not. Your office ought to be quiet as a grave. Instead your office is jumping and the plant looks like a graveyard."

Coster buried his face in his hands, then looked up. "I know it. I know what needs to be done—but every time I try to tackle a technical problem some bloody fool wants me to make a decision about trucks—or telephones—or some damn thing. I'm sorry, Mr. Harriman. I thought I could do it."

Harriman said very gently, "Don't let it throw you, Bob. You haven't had much sleep lately, have you? Tell you what—we'll put over a fast one on Ferguson. I'll take that desk you're at for a few days and build you a setup to protect you against such things. I want that brain of yours thinking about reaction vectors and fuel efficiencies and design stresses, not about contracts for trucks." Harriman stepped to the door, looked around the outer office and spotted a man who might or might not be the office's chief clerk. "Hey, you! C'mere."

The man looked startled, got up, came to the door and said, "Yes?"

"I want that desk in the corner and all the stuff that's on it moved to an empty office on this floor, right away."

The clerk raised his eyebrows. "And who are you, if I may ask?"

"Goddamn it—"

"Do as he tells you, Weber," Coster put in.

"I want it done inside of twenty minutes," added Harriman. "Jump!"

He turned back to Coster's other desk, punched the phone, and presently was speaking to the main offices of Skyways. "Jim, is your boy Jock Berkeley around? Put him on leave and send him to me, at Peterson Field, right away, special trip. I want the ship he comes in to raise ground ten minutes after we sign off. Send his gear after him." Harriman listened for a moment, then answered, "No, your organization won't fall apart if you lose Jock—or, if it does, maybe we've been paying the wrong man the top salary . . . okay, okay, you're entitled to one swift kick at my tail the next time you catch up with me, but send Jock. So long."

He supervised getting Coster and his other desk moved into another office, saw to it that the phone in the new office was disconnected, and, as an afterthought, had a couch moved in there, too. "We'll install a projector and a drafting machine and bookcases and other junk like that tonight," he told Coster. "Just make a list of anything you need—to work on *engineering*. And call me if you want anything." He went back to the nominal chief engineer's office and got happily to work trying to figure where the organization stood and what was wrong with it.

Some four hours later he took Berkeley in to meet Coster. The chief engineer was asleep at his desk, head cradled on his arms. Harriman started to back out, but Coster roused. "Oh! Sorry," he said, blushing, "I must have dozed off."

"That's why I brought you the couch," said Harriman. "It's more restful. Bob, meet Jock Berkeley. He's your new slave. You remain chief engineer and top, undisputed boss. Jock is Lord High Everything Else. From now on you've got absolutely nothing to worry about—except for the little detail of building a Moon ship."

They shook hands. "Just one thing I ask, Mr. Coster," Berkeley said seriously; "bypass me all you want to—you'll have to run the technical show—but for God's sake record it so I'll know what's going on. I'm going to have a switch placed on your desk that will operate a sealed recorder at my desk."

"Fine!" Coster was looking, Harriman thought, younger already.

"And if you want something that is not technical, don't do it yourself. Just flip a switch and whistle; it'll get done!" Berkeley glanced at Harriman. "The Boss says he wants to talk with you about the real job. I'll leave you and get busy." He left.

Harriman sat down; Coster followed suit and said, "Whew!"

"Feel better?"

"I like the looks of that fellow Berkeley."

"That's good; he's your twin brother from now on. Stop worrying; I've used him before. You'll think you're living in a well-run hospital. By the way, where do you live?"

"At a boardinghouse in the Springs."

"That's ridiculous. And you don't even have a place here to sleep?" Harriman reached over to Coster's desk, got through to Berkeley. "Jock—get a suite for Mr. Coster at the Broadmoor, under a phony name."

"Right."

"And have this stretch along here adjacent to his office fitted out as an apartment."

"Right. Tonight."

"Now, Bob, about the Moon ship. Where do we stand?"

They spent the next two hours contentedly running over the details of the problem, as Coster had laid them out. Admittedly very little work had been done since the field was leased, but Coster had accomplished considerable theoretical work and computation before he had gotten swamped in administrative details. Harriman, though no engineer and certainly not a mathematician outside the primitive arithmetic of money, had for so long devoured everything he could find about space travel that he was able to follow most of what Coster showed him.

"I don't see anything here about your mountain catapult," he said presently.

Coster looked vexed. "Oh, that! Mr. Harriman, I spoke too quickly."

"Huh? How come? I've had Montgomery's boys drawing up beautiful pictures of what things will look like when we are running regular trips. I intend to make Colorado Springs the space-port capital of the world. We hold the franchise of the old cog railroad now; what's the hitch?"

"Well, it's both time and money."

"Forget money. That's my pidgin."

"Time then. I still think an electric gun is the best way to get the initial acceleration for a chem-powered ship. Like this—" He began to sketch rapidly. "It enables you to omit the first step-rocket stage, which is bigger than all the others put together and is terribly inefficient, as it has such a poor mass ratio. But what do you have to do to get it? You can't build a tower, not a tower a couple of miles high, strong enough to take the thrusts—not this year, anyway. So you have to use a mountain. Pikes Peak is as good as any; it's accessible, at least.

"But what do you have to do to use it? First, a tunnel in through the side, from Manitou to just under the peak, and big enough to take the loaded ship—"

"Lower it down from the top," suggested Harriman.

Coster answered, "I thought of that. Elevators two miles high for loaded spaceships aren't exactly built out of string; in fact they aren't built out of any available materials. It's possible to gimmick the catapult itself so that the accelerating coils can be reversed and timed differently to do the job, but believe me, Mr. Harriman, it will throw you into other engineering problems quite as great . . . such as a giant railroad up to the top of the ship. And it still leaves you with the shaft of the catapult itself to be dug. It can't be as small as the ship, not like a gun barrel for a bullet. It's got to be considerably larger; you don't compress a column of air two miles high with impunity. Oh, a mountain catapult could be built, but it might take ten years—or longer."

"Then forget it. We'll build it for the future but not for this flight. No, wait—how about a *surface* catapult. We scoot up the side of the mountain and curve it up at the end?"

"Quite frankly, I think something like that is what will eventually be used. But, as of today, it just creates new problems. Even if we could devise an electric gun in which you could make that last curve—we can't, at present—the ship would have to be designed for terrific side stresses and all the additional weight would be parasitic so far as our main purpose is concerned, the design of a rocket ship."

"Well, Bob, what *is* your solution?"

Coster frowned. "Go back to what we know how to do—build a step rocket."

5

"Monty—"

"Yeah, Chief?"

"Have you ever heard this song?" Harriman hummed, *"The Moon belongs to everyone; the best things in life are free—"* then sang it, badly off key.

"Can't say as I ever have."

"It was before your time. I want it dug out again. I want it revived, plugged until Hell wouldn't have it, and on everybody's lips."

"Okay." Montgomery took out his memorandum pad. "When do you want it to reach its top?"

Harriman considered. "In, say, about three months. Then I want the first phrase picked up and used in advertising slogans."

"A cinch."

"How are things in Florida, Monty?"

"I thought we were going to have to buy the whole damned legislature until we got the rumor spread around that Los Angeles had contracted to have a City-Limits-of-Los-Angeles sign planted on the Moon for publicity pix. Then they came around."

"Good." Harriman pondered. "You know, that's not a bad idea. How much do you think the Chamber of Commerce of Los Angeles would pay for such a picture?"

Montgomery made another note. "I'll look into it."

"I suppose you are about ready to crank up Texas, now that Florida is loaded?"

"Most any time now. We're spreading a few snide rumors first."

Headline from Dallas-Fort Worth *Banner*:

THE MOON BELONGS TO TEXAS!!!

"—and that's all for tonight, kiddies. Don't forget to send in those box tops, or reasonable facsimiles. Remember—first prize is a thousand-acre ranch on the Moon itself, free and clear; the second prize is a six-foot scale model of the actual Moon ship, and there are fifty, count them, fifty third prizes, each a saddle-trained Shetland pony. Your hundred-word composition 'Why I want to go to the Moon' will be judged for sincerity and originality, not on literary merit. Send those box tops to Uncle Taffy, Box 214, Juarez, Old Mexico."

Harriman was shown into the office of the president of the Moka-Coka Company ("Only a Moke is truly a coke"—"Drink the Cola drink with the Lift"). He paused at the door, some twenty feet from the president's desk, and quickly pinned a two-inch-wide button to his lapel.

Patterson Griggs looked up. "Well, this is really an honor, D. D. Do come in and—" The soft-drink executive stopped suddenly, his expression changed. "What are you doing wearing *that?*" he snapped. "Trying to annoy me?"

"That" was the two-inch disc; Harriman unpinned it and put it in his pocket. It was a celluloid advertising pin, in plain yellow; printed on it in black, almost covering it, was a simple 6 +, the trademark of Moka-Coka's only serious rival.

"No," answered Harriman, "though I don't blame you for being irritated. I see half the school kids in the country wearing these silly buttons. But I came to give you a friendly tip, not to annoy you."

"What do you mean?"

"When I paused at your door that pin on my lapel was just the size—to you, standing at your desk—that the full Moon looks when you are standing in your garden, looking up at it. You didn't have any trouble reading what was on the pin, did you? I know you didn't; you yelled at me before either one of us stirred."

"What about it?"

"How would you feel—and what would the effect be on your sales—if there was 'six-plus' written across the face of the Moon instead of just on a school kid's sweater?"

Griggs thought about it, then said, "D. D., don't make poor jokes. I've had a bad day."

"I'm not joking. As you have probably heard around the Street, I'm behind this Moon trip venture. Between ourselves, Pat, it's quite an expensive undertaking, even for me. A few days ago a man came to me—you'll pardon me if I don't mention names? You can figure it out. Anyhow, this man represented a client who wanted to buy the advertising concession for the Moon. He knew we weren't sure of success, but he said his client would take the risk.

"At first I couldn't figure out what he was talking about; he set me straight. Then I thought he was kidding. Then I was shocked. Look at this—" Harriman took out a large sheet of paper and spread it on Griggs' desk. "You see the equipment is set up anywhere near the center of the Moon, as we see it. Eighteen pyrotechnics rockets shoot out in eighteen directions, like the spokes of a wheel, but to carefully calculated distances. They hit and the bombs they carry go off, spreading finely divided carbon black for calculated distances. There's no air on the Moon, you know, Pat—a fine powder will throw just as easily as a javelin. Here's your result." He turned the paper over; on the back there was a picture of the Moon, printed lightly. Overlying it, in black, heavy print was: $6 +$

"So it *is* that outfit—those poisoners!"

"No, no, I didn't say so! But it illustrates the point; six-plus is only two symbols; it can be spread large enough to be read on the face of the Moon."

Griggs stared at the horrid advertisement. "I don't believe it will work!"

"A reliable pyrotechnics firm has guaranteed that it will— provided I can deliver their equipment to the spot. After all, Pat, it doesn't take much of a pyrotechnics rocket to go a long distance on the Moon. Why, you could throw a baseball a couple of miles yourself—low gravity, you know."

"People would never stand for it. It's sacrilege!"

Harriman looked sad. "I wish you were right. But they stand for skywriting—and video commercials."

Griggs chewed his lip. "Well, I don't see why you come to me with it," he exploded. "You know damn well the name of my product won't go on the face of the Moon. The letters would be too small to be read."

Harriman nodded. "That's exactly why I came to you. Pat, this isn't just a business venture to me; it's my heart and soul. It just made me sick to think of somebody actually wanting to use the face of the Moon for advertising. As you say, it's sacrilege. But somehow, these jackals found out I was pressed for cash. They came to me when they knew I would have to listen.

"I put them off. I promised them an answer on Thursday. Then I went home and lay awake about it. After a while I thought of you."

"Me?"

"You. You and your company. After all, you've got a good product and you need legitimate advertising for it. It occurred to me that there are more ways to use the Moon in advertising than by defacing it. Now just suppose that your company bought the same concession, but with the public-spirited promise of never letting it be used. Suppose you featured that fact in your ads? Suppose you ran pictures of a boy and girl, sitting out under the Moon, sharing a bottle of Moke? Suppose Moke was the only soft drink carried on the first trip to the Moon? But I don't have to tell you how to do it." He glanced at his watch finger. "I've got to run and I don't want to rush you. If you want to do business, just leave word at my office by noon tomorrow and I'll have our man Montgomery get in touch with your advertising chief."

The head of the big newspaper chain kept him waiting the minimum time reserved for tycoons and cabinet members. Again Harriman stopped at the threshold of a large office and fixed a disc to his lapel.

"Howdy, Delos," the publisher said, "how's the traffic in green cheese today?" He then caught sight of the button and frowned. "If that is a joke, it is in poor taste."

Harriman pocketed the disc; it displayed not 6 +, but the hammer and sickle.

"No," he said, "it's not a joke; it's a nightmare. Colonel, you and I are among the few people in this country who realize that Communism is still a menace."

Sometime later they were talking as chummily as if the Colonel's chain had not obstructed the Moon venture since its inception. The publisher waved a cigar at his desk. "How did you come by those plans? Steal them?"

"They were copied," Harriman answered with narrow truth. "But they aren't important. The important thing is to get there first; we can't risk having an enemy rocket base on the Moon. For years I've had a recurrent nightmare of waking up and seeing headlines that the Russians had landed on the Moon and declared the Lunar Soviet—say thirteen men and two female scientists—and had petitioned for entrance into the U.S.S.R.—and that the petition had, of course, been graciously granted by the Supreme Soviet. I used to wake up and tremble. I don't know that they would actually go through with painting a hammer and sickle on the face of the Moon, but it's consistent with their psychology. Look at those enormous posters they are always hanging up."

The publisher bit down hard on his cigar. "We'll see what we can work out. Is there any way you can speed up your takeoff?"

6

"Mr. Harriman?"

"Yes?"

"That Mr. LeCroix is here again."

"Tell him I can't see him."

"Yes, sir—uh, Mr. Harriman, he did not mention it the other day but he says he is a rocket pilot."

"Damn it, send him around to Skyways. I don't hire pilots."

A man's face crowded into the screen, displacing Harriman's reception secretary. "Mr. Harriman—I'm Leslie LeCroix, relief pilot of the *Charon*."

"I don't care if you are the Angel Gab— Did you say *Charon?*"

"I said *Charon*. And I've got to talk to you."

"Come in."

Harriman greeted his visitor, offered him tobacco, then looked him over with interest. The *Charon*, shuttle rocket to the lost power satellite, had been the nearest thing to a spaceship the world had yet seen. Its pilot, lost in the same explosion that had destroyed the satellite and the *Charon*, had been the first, in a way, of the coming breed of spacemen.

Harriman wondered how it had escaped his attention that the *Charon* had alternating pilots. He had known it, of course—but somehow he had forgotten to take the fact into account. He had written off the power satellite, its shuttle rocket and everything about it, ceased to think about them. He now looked at LeCroix with curiosity.

He saw a small, neat man with a thin, intelligent face, and the big, competent hands of a jockey. LeCroix returned his inspection without embarrassment. He seemed calm and utterly sure of himself.

"Well, Captain LeCroix?"

"You are building a Moon ship."

"Who says so?"

"A Moon ship is being built. The boys all say you are behind it."

"Yes?"

"I want to pilot it."

"Why should you?"

"I'm the best man for it."

Harriman paused to let out a cloud of tobacco smoke. "If you can prove that, the billet is yours."

"It's a deal." LeCroix stood up. "I'll leave my name and address outside."

"Wait a minute. I said 'if.' Let's talk. I'm going along on this trip myself; I want to know more about you before I trust my neck to you."

They discussed Moon flight, interplanetary travel, rocketry, what they might find on the Moon. Gradually Harriman warmed up, as he found another spirit so like his own, so obsessed with the Wonderful Dream. Subconsciously he had already accepted LeCroix; the conversation began to assume that it would be a joint venture.

After a long time Harriman said, "This is fun, Les, but I've got to do a few chores yet today, or none of us will get to the Moon. You go on out to Peterson Field and get acquainted with Bob Coster—I'll call him. If the pair of you can manage to get along, we'll talk contract." He scribbled a chit and handed it to LeCroix. "Give this to Miss Perkins as you go out and she'll put you on the payroll."

"That can wait."

"Man's got to eat."

LeCroix accepted it but did not leave. "There's one thing I don't understand, Mr. Harriman."

"Huh?"

"Why are you planning on a chemically powered ship? Not that I object; I'll herd her. But why do it the hard way? I know you had the *City of Brisbane* refitted for X-fuel—"

Harriman stared at him. "Are you off your nut, Les? You're asking why pigs don't have wings—there isn't any X-fuel and there won't be any more until we make some ourselves—on the Moon."

"Who told you that?"

"What do you mean?"

"The way I heard it, the Atomic Energy Commission allocated X-fuel, under treaty, to several other countries—and some of them weren't prepared to make use of it. But they got it just the same. What happened to it?"

"Oh, *that!* Sure, Les, several of the little outfits in Central America and South America were cut in for a slice of pie for political reasons, even though they had no way to eat it. A good thing, too—we bought it back and used it to ease the immediate power shortage." Harriman frowned. "You're right, though. I should have grabbed some of the stuff then."

"Are you *sure* it's all gone?"

"Why, of course, I'm— No, I'm not. I'll look into it. G'bye."

His contacts were able to account for every pound of X-fuel in short order—save for Costa Rica's allotment. That nation had declined to sell back its supply because its power plant, suitable for X-fuel, had been almost finished at the time of the disaster. Another inquiry disclosed that the power plant had never been finished.

Montgomery was even then in Managua; Nicaragua had had a change in administration and Montgomery was making certain that the special position of the local Moon corporation was protected. Harriman sent him a coded message to proceed to San José, locate X-fuel, buy it and ship it back—at any cost. He then went to see the chairman of the Atomic Energy Commission.

That official was apparently glad to see him and anxious to be affable. Harriman got around to explaining that he wanted a license to do experimental work in isotopes—X-fuel, to be precise.

"This should be brought up through the usual channels, Mr. Harriman."

"It will be. This is a preliminary inquiry. I want to know your reactions."

"After all, I am not the only commissioner . . . and we almost always follow the recommendations of our technical branch."

"Don't fence with me, Carl. You know darn well you control a working majority. Off the record, what do you say?"

"Well, D. D.—off the record—you can't get any X-fuel, so why get a license?"

"Let me worry about that."

"Mmmm . . . we weren't required by law to follow every millicurie of X-fuel, since it isn't classed as potentially suitable for mass weapons. Just the same, we knew what happened to it. There's none available."

Harriman kept quiet.

"In the second place, you can have an X-fuel license, if you wish—for any purpose but rocket fuel."

"Why the restriction?"

"You are building a Moon ship, aren't you?"

"Me?"

"Don't *you* fence with *me*, D. D. It's my business to know things. You can't use X-fuel for rockets, even if you can find it —which you can't." The chairman went to a vault back of his desk and returned with a quarto volume, which he laid in front of Harriman. It was titled: *Theoretical Investigation into the Stability of Several Radioisotopic Fuels—With Notes on the* Charon-*Power-Satellite Disaster*. The cover had a serial number and was stamped: SECRET.

Harriman pushed it away. "I've got no business looking at that—and I wouldn't understand it if I did."

The chairman grinned. "Very well, I'll tell you what's in it. I'm deliberately tying your hands, D. D., by trusting you with a defense secret—"

"I won't have it, I tell you!"

"Don't try to power a spaceship with X-fuel, D. D. It's a lovely fuel—but it may go off like a firecracker anywhere out in space. That report tells why."

"Confound it, we ran the *Charon* for nearly three years!"

"You were lucky. It is the official—but utterly confidential— opinion of the government that the *Charon* set off the power satellite, rather than the satellite setting off the *Charon*. We had thought it was the other way around at first, and of course it could have been, but there was the disturbing matter of the radar records. It seemed as if the ship had gone up a split second before the satellite. So we made an intensive theoretical investigation. X-fuel is too dangerous for rockets."

"That's ridiculous! For every pound burned in the *Charon* there were at least a hundred pounds used in power plants on the surface. How come *they* didn't explode?"

"It's a matter of shielding. A rocket necessarily uses less shielding than a stationary plant, but the worst feature is that it operates out in space. The disaster is presumed to have been triggered by primary cosmic radiation. If you like, I'll call in one of the mathematical physicists to elucidate."

Harriman shook his head. "You know I don't speak the language." He considered. "I suppose that's all there is to it?"

"I'm afraid so. I'm really sorry." Harriman got up to leave. "Uh, one more thing, D. D.—you weren't thinking of approaching any of my subordinate colleagues, were you?"

"Of course not. Why should I?"

"I'm glad to hear it. You know, Mr. Harriman, some of our staff may not be the most brilliant scientists in the world—it's very hard to keep a first-class scientist happy in the conditions of government service. But there is one thing I am sure of: all of them are utterly incorruptible. Knowing that, I would take it as a personal affront if anyone tried to influence one of my people—a very personal affront."

"So?"

"Yes. By the way, I used to box light-heavyweight in college. I've kept it up."

"Hmmm . . . well, I never went to college. But I play a fair game of poker." Harriman suddenly grinned. "I won't tamper with your boys, Carl. It would be too much like offering a bribe to a starving man. Well, so long."

When Harriman got back to his office he called in one of his confidential clerks. "Take another coded message to Mr. Montgomery. Tell him to ship the stuff to Panama City, rather than to the States." He started to dictate another message to Coster, intending to tell him to stop work on the *Pioneer,* whose skeleton was already reaching skyward on the Colorado prairie, and shift to the *Santa Maria,* formerly the *City of Brisbane.*

He thought better of it. Takeoff would have to be outside the United States; with the Atomic Energy Commission acting stuffy, it would not do to try to move the *Santa Maria:* it would give the show away.

Nor could she be moved without refitting her for chem-powered flight. No, he would have another ship of the *Brisbane* class taken out of service and sent to Panama, and the power plant of the *Santa Maria* could be disassembled and shipped there, too. Coster could have the new ship ready in six weeks, maybe sooner . . . and he, Coster, and LeCroix would start for the Moon!

The devil with worries over primary cosmic rays! The *Charon* operated for three years, didn't she? They would make the trip, they would prove it could be done, then, if safer fuels were needed, there would be the incentive to dig them out. The important thing was to do it, make the trip. If Columbus had waited for decent ships, we'd all still be in Europe. A man had to take some chances or he never got anywhere.

Contentedly he started drafting the messages that would get the new scheme under way.

He was interrupted by a secretary. "Mr. Harriman, Mr. Montgomery wants to speak to you."

"Eh? Has he gotten my code already?"

"I don't know, sir."

"Well, put him on."

Montgomery had not received the second message. But he had news for Harriman: Costa Rica had sold all its X-fuel to the English Ministry of Power, soon after the disaster. There was not an ounce of it left, neither in Costa Rica, nor in England.

Harriman sat and moped for several minutes after Montgomery had cleared the screen. Then he called Coster. "Bob? Is LeCroix there?"

"Right here—we were about to go out to dinner together. Here he is, now."

"Howdy, Les. Les, that was a good brain storm of yours, but it didn't work. Somebody stole the baby."

"Eh? Oh, I get you. I'm sorry."

"Don't ever waste time being sorry. We'll go ahead as originally planned. We'll get there!"

"Sure we will."

7

From the June issue of *Popular Technics* magazine: "URANIUM PROSPECTING ON THE MOON—a Fact Article about a soon-to-come Major Industry."

From *Holiday:* "Honeymoon on the Moon—A Discussion of the Miracle Resort that your children will enjoy, as told to our travel editor."

From the *American Sunday Magazine:* "DIAMONDS ON THE MOON?—A World-Famous Scientist Shows Why Diamonds Must Be Common as Pebbles in the Lunar Craters."

"Of course, Clem, I don't know anything about electronics, but here is the way it was explained to me. You can hold the beam of a television broadcast down to a degree or so these days, can't you?"

"Yes—if you use a big enough reflector."

"You'll have plenty of elbowroom. Now Earth covers a space two degrees wide, as seen from the Moon. Sure, it's quite a distance away, but you'd have no power losses and absolutely perfect and unchanging conditions for transmission. Once you made your setup, it wouldn't be any more expensive than broadcasting from the top of a mountain here, and a darned sight less expensive than keeping copters in the air from coast to coast, the way you're having to do now."

"It's a fantastic scheme, Delos."

"What's fantastic about it? Getting to the Moon is my worry, not yours. Once we are there, there's going to be television back to Earth, you can bet your shirt on that. It's a natural setup for line-of-sight transmission. If you aren't interested, I'll have to find someone who is."

"I didn't say I wasn't interested."

"Well, make up your mind. Here's another thing, Clem—I don't want to go sticking my nose into your business, but haven't you had a certain amount of trouble since you lost the use of the power satellite as a relay station?"

"You know the answer; don't needle me. Expenses have gone out of sight without any improvement in revenue."

"That wasn't quite what I meant. How about censorship?"

The television executive threw up his hands. "Don't say that word! How anybody expects a man to stay in business with every two-bit wowser in the country claiming a veto over what we can say and can't say and what we can show and what we can't show—it's enough to make you throw up. The whole principle is wrong; it's like demanding that grown men live on skim milk because the baby can't eat steak. If I were able to lay my hands on those confounded, prurient-minded, slimy—"

"Easy! Easy!" Harriman interrupted. "Did it ever occur to you that there is absolutely no way to interfere with a telecast from the Moon—and that boards of censorship on Earth won't have jurisdiction in any case?"

"What? Say that again."

" 'LIFE goes to the Moon.' Time-Life Inc. is proud to announce that arrangements have been completed to bring *Life*'s readers a personally conducted tour of the first trip to our satellite. In place of the usual weekly feature 'LIFE

Goes to a Party' there will commence, immediately after the return of the first successful—"

"ASSURANCE FOR THE NEW AGE"

(An excerpt from an advertisement of the North Atlantic Mutual Insurance and Liability Company)

"—the same looking-to-the-future that protected our policyholders after the Chicago Fire, after the San Francisco Fire, after every disaster since the War of 1812, now reaches out to insure you from unexpected loss *even on the Moon*—"

"THE UNBOUNDED FRONTIERS OF TECHNOLOGY"

"When the Moon ship *Pioneer* climbs skyward on a ladder of flame, twenty-seven essential devices in her 'innard's will be powered by especially engineered DELTA batteries—"

"Mr. Harriman, could you come out to the field?"

"What's up, Bob?"

"Trouble," Coster answered briefly.

"What sort of trouble?"

Coster hesitated. "I'd rather not talk about it by screen. If you can't come, maybe Les and I had better come there."

"I'll be there this evening."

When Harriman got there he saw that LeCroix's impassive face concealed bitterness, Coster looked stubborn and defensive. He waited until the three were alone in Coster's workroom before he spoke. "Let's have it, boys."

LeCroix looked at Coster. The engineer chewed his lip and said, "Mr. Harriman, you know the stages this design has been through."

"More or less."

"We had to give up the catapult idea. Then we had this—" Coster rummaged on his desk, pulled out a perspective treatment of a four-step rocket, large but rather graceful. "Theoretically it was a possibility; practically it cut things too fine. By the time the stress group boys and the auxiliary group and the control group got through adding things we were forced to come to this—" He hauled out another sketch; it was basically like the first, but squatter, almost pyramidal. "We added a fifth stage as a ring around the fourth stage. We even managed to save some weight by using most of the auxiliary and control equipment for the fourth stage to control the fifth stage. And it still had enough sectional density to punch through the atmosphere with no important drag, even if it was clumsy."

Harriman nodded. "You know, Bob, we're going to have to get away from the step rocket idea before we set up a scheduled run to the Moon."

"I don't see how you can avoid it with chem-powered rockets."

"If you had a decent catapult you could put a single-stage chem-powered rocket into an orbit around the Earth, couldn't you?"

"Sure."

"That's what we'll do. Then it will refuel in that orbit."

"The old space-station setup. I suppose that makes sense—in fact I know it does. Only the ship wouldn't refuel and continue on to the Moon. The economical thing would be to have special ships that never landed anywhere make the jump from there to another fueling station around the Moon. Then—"

LeCroix displayed a most unusual impatience. "All that doesn't mean anything now. Get on with the story, Bob."

"Right," agreed Harriman.

"Well, this model should have done it. And, damn it, it still should do it."

Harriman looked puzzled. "But, Bob, that's the approved design, isn't it? That's what you've got two-thirds built right out there on the field."

"Yes." Coster looked stricken. "But it won't do it. It won't work."

"Why not?"

"Because I've had to add in too much dead weight, that's why. Mr. Harriman, you aren't an engineer; you've no idea how fast the performance falls off when you have to clutter up a ship with anything but fuel and power plant. Take the landing arrangements for the fifth-stage power ring. You use that stage for a minute and a half, then you throw it away. But you don't dare take a chance of it falling on Wichita or Kansas City. We have to include a parachute sequence. Even then we have to plan on tracking it by radar and cutting the shrouds by radio control when it's over empty countryside and not too high. That means more weight, besides the parachute. By the time we are through, we don't get a net addition of a mile a second out of that stage. It's not enough."

Harriman stirred in his chair. "Looks like we made a mistake in trying to launch it from the States. Suppose we took off from someplace unpopulated, say the Brazil coast, and let the booster stages fall in the Atlantic; how much would that save you?"

Coster looked off in the distance, then took out a slide rule. "Might work."

"How much of a chore will it be to move the ship, at this stage?"

"Well . . . it would have to be disassembled completely; nothing less would do. I can't give you a cost estimate offhand, but it would be expensive."

"How long would it take?"

"Hmm . . . shucks, Mr. Harriman, I can't answer offhand. Two years—eighteen months, with luck. We'd have to prepare a site. We'd have to build shops."

Harriman thought about it, although he knew the answer in his heart. His shoestring, big as it was, was stretched to the danger point. He couldn't keep up the promotion, on talk alone, for another two years; he *had* to have a successful flight and soon —or the whole jerry-built financial structure would burst. "No good, Bob."

"I was afraid of that. Well, I tried to add still a sixth stage."
He held up another sketch. "You see that monstrosity? I reached
the point of diminishing returns. The final effective velocity is
actually less with this abortion than with the five-step job."

"Does that mean you are whipped, Bob? You can't build a
Moon ship?"

"No, I—"

LeCroix said suddenly, "Clear out Kansas."

"Eh?" asked Harriman.

"Clear everybody out of Kansas and Eastern Colorado. Let
the fifth and fourth sections fall anywhere in that area. The
third section falls in the Atlantic; the second section goes into a
permanent orbit—and the ship itself goes on to the Moon. You
could do it if you didn't have to waste weight on the para-
chuting of the fifth and fourth sections. Ask Bob."

"So? How about it, Bob?"

"That's what I said before. It was the parasitic penalties that
whipped us. The basic design is all right."

"Hmmm . . . somebody hand me an atlas." Harriman
looked up Kansas and Colorado, did some rough figuring. He
stared off into space, looking surprisingly, for the moment, as
Coster did when the engineer was thinking about his own work.
Finally he said, "It won't work."

"Why not?"

"Money. I told you not to worry about money—for the ship.
But it would cost upward of six or seven million dollars to evac-
uate that area even for a day. We'd have to settle nuisance suits
out of hand; we couldn't wait. And there would be a few die-
hards who just couldn't move anyhow."

LeCroix said savagely, "If the crazy fools won't move, let
them take their chances."

"I know how you feel, Les. But this project is too big to hide
and too big to move. Unless we protect the bystanders we'll be
shut down by court order and force. I can't buy all the judges
in two states. Some of them wouldn't be for sale."

"It was a nice try, Les," consoled Coster.

"I thought it might be an answer for all of us," the pilot answered.

Harriman said, "You were starting to mention another solution, Bob?"

Coster looked embarrassed. "You know the plans for the ship itself—a three-man job, space and supplies for three."

"Yes. What are you driving at?"

"It doesn't have to be three men. Split the first step into two parts, cut the ship down to the bare minimum for one man and jettison the remainder. That's the only way I see to make this basic design work." He got out another sketch. "See? One man and supplies for less than a week. No airlock—the pilot stays in his pressure suit. No galley. No bunks. The bare minimum to keep one man alive for a maximum of two hundred hours. It will work."

"It will work," repeated LeCroix, looking at Coster.

Harriman looked at the sketch with an odd, sick feeling at his stomach. Yes, no doubt it would work—and for the purposes of the promotion it did not matter whether one man or three went to the Moon and returned. Just to do it was enough; he was dead certain that one successful flight would cause money to roll in so that there would be capital to develop to the point of practical, passenger-carrying ships.

The Wright brothers had started with less.

"If that is what I have to put up with, I suppose I have to," he said slowly.

Coster looked relieved. "Fine! But there is one more hitch. You know the conditions under which I agreed to tackle this job—I was to go along. Now Les here waves a contract under my nose and says *he* has to be the pilot."

"It's not just that," LeCroix countered. "You're no pilot, Bob. You'll kill yourself and ruin the whole enterprise, just through bullheaded stubbornness."

"I'll learn to fly it. After all, I designed it. Look here, Mr.

Harriman, I hate to let you in for a suit—Les says he will sue—but my contract antedates his. I intend to enforce it."

"Don't listen to him, Mr. Harriman. Let him do the suing. I'll fly that ship and bring her back. He'll wreck it."

"Either I go or I don't build the ship," Coster said flatly.

Harriman motioned both of them to keep quiet. "Easy, easy, both of you. You can both sue me if it gives you any pleasure. Bob, don't talk nonsense; at this stage I can hire other engineers to finish the job. You tell me it has to be just one man."

"That's right."

"You're looking at him."

They both stared.

"Shut your jaws," Harriman snapped. "What's funny about that? You both knew I meant to go. You don't think I went to all this trouble just to give you two a ride to the Moon, do you? *I intend to go.* What's wrong with me as a pilot? I'm in good health, my eyesight is all right, I'm still smart enough to learn what I have to learn. If I have to drive my own buggy, I'll do it. I won't step aside for anybody, not anybody, d'you hear me?"

Coster got his breath first. "Boss, you don't know what you are saying."

Two hours later they were still wrangling. Most of the time Harriman had stubbornly sat still, refusing to answer their arguments. At last he went out of the room for a few minutes, on the usual pretext. When he came back in he said, "Bob, what do you weigh?"

"Me? A little over two hundred."

"Close to two twenty, I'd judge. Les, what do you weigh?"

"One twenty-six."

"Bob, design the ship for a net load of one hundred and twenty-six pounds."

"Huh? Now wait a minute, Mr. Harriman—"

"*Shut up!* If I can't learn to be a pilot in six weeks, neither can you."

"But I've got the mathematics and the basic knowledge to—"

"Shut up I said! Les has spent as long learning his profession as you have learning yours. Can he become an engineer in six weeks? Then what gave you the conceit to think that you can learn his job in that time? I'm not going to have you wrecking my ship to satisfy your swollen ego. Anyhow, you gave out the real key to it when you were discussing the design. The real limiting factor is the actual weight of the passenger or passengers, isn't it? Everything—*everything* works in proportion to that one mass. Right?"

"Yes, but—"

"Right or wrong?"

"Well . . . yes, that's right. I just wanted—"

"The smaller man can live on less water, he breathes less air, he occupies less space. Les goes." Harriman walked over and put a hand on Coster's shoulder. "Don't take it hard, son. It can't be any worse on you than it is on me. This trip has got to succeed—and that means you and I have got to give up the honor of being the first man on the Moon. But I promise you this: we'll go on the second trip, we'll go with Les as our private chauffeur. It will be the first of a lot of passenger trips. Look, Bob—you can be a big man in this game, if you'll play along now. How would you like to be chief engineer of the first lunar colony?"

Coster managed to grin. "It might not be so bad."

"You'd like it. Living on the Moon will be an engineering problem; you and I have talked about it. How'd you like to put your theories to work? Build the first city? Build the big observatory we'll found there? Look around and know that you were the man who had done it?"

Coster was definitely adjusting himself to it. "You make it sound good. Say, what will *you* be doing."

"Me? Well, maybe I'll be the first mayor of Luna City." It was a new thought to him; he savored it. "The Honorable Delos

David Harriman, Mayor of Luna City. Say, I like that! You
know, I've never held any sort of public office; I've just owned
things." He looked around. "Everything settled?"

"I guess so," Coster said slowly. Suddenly he stuck his hand
out at LeCroix. "You fly her, Les; I'll build her."

LeCroix grabbed his hand. "It's a deal. And you and the Boss
get busy and start making plans for the next job—big enough
for all of us."

"Right!"

Harriman put his hand on top of theirs. "That's the way I like
to hear you talk. We'll stick together and we'll found Luna City
together."

"I think we ought to call it 'Harriman,'" LeCroix said
seriously.

"Nope, I've thought of it as Luna City ever since I was a kid;
Luna City it's going to be. Maybe we'll put Harriman Square in
the middle of it," he added.

"I'll mark it that way in the plans," agreed Coster.

Harriman left at once. Despite the solution he was terribly
depressed and did not want his two colleagues to see it. It had
been a Pyrrhic victory; he had saved the enterprise but he felt
like an animal who has gnawed off his own leg to escape a trap.

8

Strong was alone in the offices of the partnership when he
got a call from Dixon. "George, I was looking for D. D. Is he
there?"

"No, he's back in Washington—something about clearances.
I expect him back soon."

"Hmmm . . . . Entenza and I want to see him. We're coming over."

They arrived shortly. Entenza was quite evidently very much
worked up over something; Dixon looked sleekly impassive as

usual. After greetings Dixon waited a moment, then said, "Jack, you had some business to transact, didn't you?"

Entenza jumped, then snatched a draft from his pocket. "Oh, yes! George, I'm not going to have to prorate after all. Here's my payment to bring my share up to full payment to date."

Strong accepted it. "I know that Delos will be pleased." He tucked it in a drawer.

"Well," said Dixon sharply, "aren't you going to receipt for it?"

"If Jack wants a receipt. The canceled draft will serve." However, Strong wrote out a receipt without further comment; Entenza accepted it.

They waited a while. Presently Dixon said, "George, you're in this pretty deep, aren't you?"

"Possibly."

"Want to hedge your bets?"

"How?"

"Well, candidly, I want to protect myself. Want to sell me half of one percent of your share?"

Strong thought about it. In fact he was worried—worried sick. The presence of Dixon's auditor had forced them to keep on a cash basis—and only Strong knew how close to the line that had forced the partners.

"Why do you want it?"

"Oh, I wouldn't use it to interfere with Delos' operations. He's our man; we're backing him. But I would feel a lot safer if I had the right to call a halt if he tried to commit us to something we couldn't pay for. You know Delos; he's an incurable optimist. We ought to have some sort of a brake on him."

Strong thought about it. The thing that hurt him was that he agreed with everything Dixon said; he had stood by and watched while Delos dissipated two fortunes, painfully built up through the years. D. D. no longer seemed to care. Why, only this morning he had refused even to look at a report on the H&S automatic household switch—after dumping it on Strong.

Dixon leaned forward. "Name a price, George. I'll be generous."

Strong squared his stooped shoulders. "I'll sell—"

"Good!"

"—if Delos okays it. Not otherwise."

Dixon muttered something. Entenza snorted. The conversation might have gone acrimoniously further had not Harriman walked in.

No one said anything about the proposal to Strong. Strong inquired about the trip; Harriman pressed a thumb and finger together. "All in the groove! But it gets more expensive to do business in Washington every day." He turned to the others. "How's tricks? Any special meaning to the assemblage? Are we in executive session?"

Dixon turned to Entenza. "Tell him, Jack."

Entenza faced Harriman. "What do you mean by selling television rights?"

Harriman cocked a brow. "And why not?"

"Because you promised them to me, that's why. That's the original agreement; I've got it in writing."

"Better take another look at the agreement, Jack. And don't go off half-cocked. You have the exploitation rights for radio, television, and other amusement and special feature ventures in connection with the first trip to the Moon. You've still got 'em. Including broadcasts from the ship, provided we are able to make any." He decided that this was not a good time to mention that weight considerations had already made the latter impossible; the *Pioneer* would carry no electronic equipment of any sort not needed in astrogation. "What I sold was the franchise to erect a television station on the Moon, later. By the way, it wasn't even an exclusive franchise, although Clem Haggerty thinks it is. If you want to buy one yourself, we can accommodate you."

"*Buy* it! Why, you—"

"Wups! Or you can have it free, if you can get Dixon and

George to agree that you are entitled to it. I won't be a tight-wad. Anything else?"

Dixon cut in. "Just where do we stand now, Delos?"

"Gentlemen, you can take it for granted that the *Pioneer* will leave on schedule—next Wednesday. And now, if you will excuse me, I'm on my way to Peterson Field."

After he had left, his three associates sat in silence for some time, Entenza muttering to himself, Dixon apparently thinking, and Strong just waiting. Presently Dixon said, "How about that fractional share, George?"

"You didn't see fit to mention it to Delos."

"I see." Dixon carefully deposited an ash. "He's a strange man, isn't he?"

Strong shifted around. "Yes."

"How long have you known him?"

"Let me see—he came to work for me in—"

"*He* worked for *you?*"

"For several months. Then we set up our first company." Strong thought back about it. "I suppose he had a power complex, even then."

"No," Dixon said carefully. "No, I wouldn't call it a power complex. It's more of a Messiah complex."

Entenza looked up. "He's a crooked son of a bitch, that's what he is!"

Strong looked at him mildly. "I'd rather you wouldn't talk about him that way. I'd really rather you wouldn't."

"Stow it, Jack," ordered Dixon. "You might force George to take a poke at you. One of the odd things about him," went on Dixon, "is that he seems to be able to inspire an almost feudal loyalty. Take yourself. I know you are cleaned out, George—yet you won't let me rescue you. That goes beyond logic; it's personal."

Strong nodded. "He's an odd man. Sometimes I think he's the last of the Robber Barons."

Dixon shook his head. "Not the last. The last of them opened up the American West. He's the first of the *new* Robber Barons —and you and I won't see the end of it. Do you ever read Carlyle?"

Strong nodded again. "I see what you mean, the 'Hero' theory, but I don't necessarily agree with it."

"There's something to it, though," Dixon answered. "Truthfully, I don't think Delos knows what he is doing. He's setting up a new imperialism. There'll be hell to pay before it's cleaned up." He stood up. "Maybe we should have waited. Maybe we should have balked him—*if* we could have. Well, it's done. We're on the merry-go-round and we can't get off. I hope we enjoy the ride. Come on, Jack."

9

The Colorado Prairie was growing dusky. The Sun was behind the peak and the broad white face of Luna, full and round, was rising in the east. In the middle of Peterson Field the *Pioneer* thrust toward the sky. A barbed-wire fence, a thousand yards from its base in all directions, held back the crowds. Just inside the barrier, guards patrolled restlessly. More guards circulated through the crowd. Inside the fence, close to it, trucks and trailers for camera, sound, and television equipment were parked and, at the far ends of cables, remote-control pickups were located both near and far from the ship on all sides. There were other trucks near the ship and a stir of organized activity.

Harriman waited in Coster's office; Coster himself was out on the field, and Dixon and Entenza had a room to themselves. LeCroix, still in a drugged sleep, was in the bedroom of Coster's on-the-job living quarters.

There was a stir and a challenge outside the door. Harriman opened it a crack. "If that's another reporter, tell him 'no.' Send him to Mr. Montgomery across the way. Captain LeCroix will grant no unauthorized interviews."

"Delos! Let me in."

"Oh—you, George. Come in. We've been hounded to death."

Strong came in and handed Harriman a large and heavy handbag. "Here it is."

"Here is what?"

"The canceled covers for the philatelic syndicate. You forgot them. That's half a million dollars, Delos," he complained. "If I hadn't noticed them in your coat locker we'd have been in the soup."

Harriman composed his features. "George, you're a brick, that's what you are."

"Shall I put them in the ship myself?" Strong said anxiously.

"Huh? No, no. Les will handle them." He glanced at his watch. "We're about to waken him. I'll take charge of the covers." He took the bag and added, "Don't come in now. You'll have a chance to say goodbye on the field."

Harriman went next door, shut the door behind him, waited for the nurse to give the sleeping pilot a counteracting stimulant by injection, then chased her out. When he turned around the pilot was sitting up, rubbing his eyes. "How do you feel, Les?"

"Fine. So this is it."

"Yup. And we're all rooting for you, boy. Look, you've got to go out and face them in a couple of minutes. Everything is ready—but I've got a couple of things I've got to say to you."

"Yes?"

"See this bag?" Harriman rapidly explained what it was and what it signified.

LeCroix looked dismayed. "But I *can't* take it, Delos. It's all figured to the last ounce."

"Who said you were going to take it? Of course you can't; it must weigh sixty, seventy pounds. I just plain forgot it. Now here's what we do: for the time being I'll just hide it in here—" Harriman stuffed the bag far back into a clothes closet. "When you land, I'll be right on your tail. Then we pull a sleight-of-hand trick and you fetch it out of the ship."

LeCroix shook his head ruefully. "Delos, you beat me. Well, I'm in no mood to argue."

"I'm glad you're not; otherwise I'd go to jail for a measly half million dollars. We've already spent that money. Anyhow, it doesn't matter," he went on. "Nobody but you and me will know it—and the stamp collectors will get their money's worth." He looked at the younger man as if anxious for his approval.

"Okay, okay," LeCroix answered. "Why should I care what happens to a stamp collector—tonight? Let's get going."

"One more thing," said Harriman and took out a small cloth bag. "This you take with you—and the weight *has* been figured in. I saw to it. Now here is what you do with it." He gave detailed and very earnest instructions.

LeCroix was puzzled. "Do I hear you straight? I let it be found—then I tell the exact truth about what happened?"

"That's right."

"Okay." LeCroix zipped the little bag into a pocket of his coveralls. "Let's get out to the field. H-hour minus twenty-one minutes already."

Strong joined Harriman in the control blockhouse after LeCroix had gone up inside the ship. "Did they get aboard?" he demanded anxiously. "LeCroix wasn't carrying anything."

"Oh, sure," said Harriman. "I sent them ahead. Better take your place. The ready flare has already gone up."

Dixon, Entenza, the Governor of Colorado, the Vice-President of the United States, and a round dozen of VIP's were already seated at periscopes, mounted in slits, on a balcony above the control level. Strong and Harriman climbed a ladder and took the two remaining chairs.

Harriman began to sweat and realized he was trembling. Through his periscope out in front he could see the ship; from below he could hear Coster's voice, nervously checking departure station reports. Muted through a speaker by him was a running commentary of one of the newscasters reporting the show. Harriman himself was the—well, the admiral, he decided—of the operation, but there was nothing more he could do but wait, watch, and try to pray.

A second flare arched up in the sky, burst into red and green. Five minutes.

The seconds oozed away. At minus two minutes Harriman realized that he could not stand to watch through a tiny slit; he had to be outside, take part in it himself—he had to. He climbed down, hurried to the exit of the blockhouse. Coster glanced around, looked startled, but did not try to stop him; Coster could not leave his post no matter what happened. Harriman elbowed the guard aside and went outdoors.

To the east the ship towered skyward, her slender pyramid sharp black against the full Moon. He waited.

And waited.

What had gone wrong? There had remained less than two minutes when he had come out; he was sure of that—yet there she stood, silent, dark, unmoving. There was not a sound, save the distant ululation of sirens warning the spectators behind the distant fence. Harriman felt his own heart stop, his breath dry up in his throat. Something had failed. Failure.

A single flare rocket burst from the top of the blockhouse; a flame licked at the base of the ship.

It spread, there was a pad of white fire around the base. Slowly, almost lumberingly, the *Pioneer* lifted, seemed to hover for a moment, balanced on a pillar of fire—then reached for the sky with acceleration so great that she was above him almost at once, overhead at the zenith, a dazzling circle of flame. So quickly was she above, rather than out in front, that it seemed as if she were arching back over him and must surely fall on him. Instinctively and futilely he threw a hand in front of his face.

The sound reached him.

Not as sound—it was a white noise, a roar in all frequencies, sonic, subsonic, supersonic, so incredibly loaded with energy that it struck him in the chest. He heard it with his teeth and with his bones as well as with his ears. He crouched his knees, bracing against it.

Following the sound at the snail's pace of a hurricane came the backwash of the splash. It ripped at his clothing, tore his breath from his lips. He stumbled blindly back, trying to reach the lee of the concrete building, was knocked down.

He picked himself up coughing and strangling and remembered to look at the sky. Straight overhead was a dwindling star. Then it was gone.

He went into the blockhouse.

The room was a babble of high-tension, purposeful confusion. Harriman's ears, still ringing, heard a speaker blare, "Spot One! Spot One to Blockhouse! Step five loose on schedule—ship and step five showing separate blips—" and Coster's voice, high and angry, cutting in with, "Get Track One! Have they picked up step five yet? Are they tracking it?"

In the background the news commentator was still blowing his top. "A great day, folks, a great day! The mighty *Pioneer*, climbing like an angel of the Lord, flaming sword at hand, is even now on her glorious way to our sister planet. Most of you have seen her departure on your screens; I wish you could have seen it as I did, arching up into the evening sky, bearing her precious load of—"

"Shut that damn thing off!" ordered Coster, then to the visitors on the observation platform, "And pipe down up there! Quiet!"

The Vice-President of the United States jerked his head around, closed his mouth. He remembered to smile. The other VIP's shut up, then resumed again in muted whispers. A girl's voice cut through the silence, "Track One to Blockhouse—step five tracking high, plus two." There was a stir in the corner. There a large canvas hood shielded a heavy sheet of Plexiglas from direct light. The sheet was mounted vertically and was edge-lighted; it displayed a coordinate map of Colorado and Kansas in fine white lines; the cities and towns glowed red. Unevacuated farms were tiny warning dots of red light.

A man behind the transparent map touched it with a grease pencil; the reported location of step five shone out. In front of the map screen a youngish man sat quietly in a chair, a pear-shaped switch in his hand, his thumb lightly resting on the button. He was a bombardier, borrowed from the Air Forces; when he pressed the switch, a radio-controlled circuit in step five should cause the shrouds of step five's landing chute to be cut and let it plummet to Earth. He was working from radar reports alone with no fancy computing bombsight to think for him. He was working almost by instinct—or, rather, by the accumulated subconscious knowledge of his trade, integrating in his brain the meager data spread before him, deciding where the tons of step five would land if he were to press his switch at any particular instant. He seemed unworried.

"Spot One to Blockhouse!" came a man's voice again. "Step four free on schedule," and almost immediately following, a deeper voice echoed, "Track Two, tracking step four, instantaneous altitude nine-five-one miles, predicted vector."

No one paid any attention to Harriman.

Under the hood the observed trajectory of step five grew in shining dots of grease, near to, but not on, the dotted line of its predicted path. Reaching out from each location dot was drawn a line at right angles, the reported altitude for that location.

The quiet man watching the display suddenly pressed down hard on his switch. He then stood up, stretched, and said, "Anybody got a cigarette?" "Track Two!" he was answered. "Step four—first impact prediction—forty miles west of Charleston, South Carolina."

"Repeat!" yelled Coster.

The speaker blared out again without pause, "Correction, correction—forty miles east, repeat *east*."

Coster sighed. The sigh was cut short by a report: "Spot One to Blockhouse—step three free, minus five seconds," and a talker at Coster's control desk called out, "Mr. Coster, *Mister Coster*—Palomar Observatory wants to talk to you."

"Tell 'em to go—no, tell 'em to wait." Immediately another voice cut in with, "Track One, auxiliary range Fox—Step One about to strike near Dodge City, Kansas."

"How near!"

There was no answer. Presently the voice of Track One proper said, "Impact reported approximately fifteen miles southwest of Dodge City."

"Casualties?"

Spot One broke in before Track One could answer, "Step two free, step two free—the ship is now on its own."

"Mr. Coster—*please*, Mr. Coster—"

And a totally new voice: "Spot Two to Blockhouse—we are now tracking the ship. Stand by for reported distances and bearings. Stand by—"

"Track Two to Blockhouse—step four will definitely land in Atlantic, estimated point of impact oh-five-seven miles east of Charleston bearing oh-nine-three. I will repeat—"

Coster looked around irritably. "Isn't there any drinking water anywhere in this dump?"

"Mr. Coster, please—Palomar says they've just *got* to talk to you."

Harriman eased over to the door and stepped out. He suddenly felt very much let down, utterly weary, and depressed.

The field looked strange without the ship. He had watched it grow; now suddenly it was gone. The Moon, still rising, seemed oblivious—and space travel was as remote a dream as it had been in his boyhood.

There were several tiny figures prowling around the flash apron where the ship had stood—souvenir hunters, he thought contemptuously. Someone came up to him in the gloom. "Mr. Harriman?"

"Eh?"

"Hopkins—with the A.P. How about a statement?"

"Uh? No, no comment. I'm bushed."

"Oh, now, just a word. How does it feel to have backed the first successful Moon flight—if it is successful."

"It will be successful." He thought a moment, then squared his tired shoulders and said, "Tell them that this is the beginning of the human race's greatest era. Tell them that every one of them will have a chance to follow in Captain LeCroix's footsteps, seek out new planets, wrest a home for themselves in new lands. Tell them that this means new frontiers, a shot in the arm for prosperity. It means—" He ran down. "That's all tonight. I'm whipped, son. Leave me alone, will you?"

Presently Coster came out, followed by the VIP's. Harriman went up to Coster. "Everything all right?"

"Sure. Why shouldn't it be? Track Three followed him out to the limit of range—all in the groove." Coster added, "Step five killed a cow when it grounded."

"Forget it—we'll have steak for breakfast." Harriman then had to make conversation with the Governor and the Vice-President, had to escort them out to their ship. Dixon and Entenza left together, less formally; at last Coster and Harriman were alone save for subordinates too junior to constitute a strain and for guards to protect them from the crowds. "Where you headed, Bob?"

"Up to the Broadmoor and about a week's sleep. How about you?"

"If you don't mind, I'll doss down in your apartment."

"Help yourself. Sleepy pills in the bathroom."

"I won't need them." They had a drink together in Coster's quarters, talked aimlessly, then Coster ordered a copter cab and went to the hotel. Harriman went to bed, got up, read a day-old copy of the Denver *Post* filled with pictures of the *Pioneer*, finally gave up and took two of Coster's sleeping capsules.

10

Someone was shaking him. "Mr. Harriman! Wake up—Mr. Coster is on the screen."

"Huh? Wazza? Oh, all right." He got up and padded to the phone. Coster was looking tousleheaded and excited. "Hey, Boss—*he made it!*"

"Huh? What do you mean?"

"Palomar just called me. They saw his mark and now they've spotted the ship itself. He—"

"Wait a minute, Bob. Slow up. He *can't* be there yet. He just left last night."

Coster looked disconcerted. "What's the matter, Mr. Harriman? Don't you feel well? He left Wednesday."

Vaguely, Harriman began to be oriented. No, the takeoff had not been the night before—fuzzily he recalled a drive up into the mountains, a day spent dozing in the sun, some sort of a party at which he had drunk too much. What day was today? He didn't know. If LeCroix had landed on the Moon, then— never mind. "It's all right, Bob—I was half asleep. I guess I dreamed the takeoff all over again. Now tell me the news, slowly."

Coster started over. "LeCroix has landed, just west of Archimedes crater. They can see his ship, from Palomar. Say that was a great stunt you thought up, marking the spot with carbon black. Les must have covered two acres with it. They say it shines out like a billboard, through the Big Eye."

"Maybe we ought to run down and have a look. No—later," he amended. "We'll be busy."

"I don't see what more we can do, Mr. Harriman. We've got twelve of our best ballistic computers calculating possible routes for you now."

Harriman started to tell the man to put on another twelve, switched off the screen instead. He was still at Peterson Field, with one of Skyways' best stratoships waiting for him outside, waiting to take him to whatever point on the globe LeCroix might ground. LeCroix was in the upper stratosphere, had been there for more than twenty-four hours. The pilot was slowly, cautiously wearing out his terminal velocity, dissipating the incredible kinetic energy as shock wave and radiant heat.

They had tracked him by radar around the globe and around again—and again . . . yet there was no way of knowing just where and what sort of landing the pilot would choose to risk. Harriman listened to the running radar reports and cursed the fact that they had elected to save the weight of radio equipment.

The radar figures started coming closer together. The voice broke off and started again: "He's in his landing glide!"

"Tell the field to get ready!" shouted Harriman. He held his breath and waited. After endless seconds another voice cut in with, "The Moon ship is now landing. It will ground somewhere west of Chihuahua in Old Mexico."

Harriman started for the door at a run.

Coached by radio en route, Harriman's pilot spotted the *Pioneer* incredibly small against the desert sand. He put his own ship quite close to it, in a beautiful landing. Harriman was fumbling at the cabin door before the ship was fairly stopped.

LeCroix was sitting on the ground, resting his back against a skid of his ship and enjoying the shade of its stubby triangular wings. A paisano sheepherder stood facing him, open-mouthed. As Harriman trotted out and lumbered toward him LeCroix stood up, flipped a cigarette butt away and said, "Hi, Boss!"

"Les!" The older man threw his arms around the younger. "It's good to see you, boy."

"It's good to see *you*. Pedro here doesn't speak my language." LeCroix glanced around; there was no one else nearby but the pilot of Harriman's ship. "Where's the gang? Where's Bob?"

"I didn't wait. They'll surely be along in a few minutes—hey, there they come now!" It was another stratoship, plunging in to a landing. Harriman turned to his pilot. "Bill—go over and meet them."

"Huh? They'll come, never fear."

"Do as I say."

"You're the doctor." The pilot trudged through the sand, his back expressing disapproval. LeCroix looked puzzled. "Quick, Les—help me with this."

"This" was the five thousand canceled envelopes which were supposed to have been to the Moon. They got them out of Harriman's stratoship and into the Moon ship, there to be stowed in an empty food locker, while their actions were still shielded from the later arrivals by the bulk of the stratoship.

"Whew!" said Harriman. "That was close. Half a million dollars. We need it, Les."

"Sure, but look, Mr. Harriman, the di—"

"Sssh! The others are coming. How about the other business? Ready with your act?"

"Yes. But I was trying to tell you—"

"Quiet!"

It was not their colleagues; it was a shipload of reporters, cameramen, mike men, commentators, technicians. They swarmed over them.

Harriman waved to them jauntily. "Help yourselves, boys. Get a lot of pictures. Climb through the ship. Make yourselves at home. Look at anything you want to. But go easy on Captain LeCroix—he's tired."

Another ship had landed, this time with Coster, Dixon and Strong. Entenza showed up in his own chartered ship and began bossing the TV, pix, and radiomen, in the course of which he almost had a fight with an unauthorized camera crew. A large copter transport grounded and spilled out nearly a platoon of khaki-clad Mexican troops. From somewhere—out of the sand apparently—several dozen native peasants showed up. Harriman broke away from reporters, held a quick and expensive discussion with the captain of the local troops and a degree of order was restored in time to save the *Pioneer* from being picked to pieces.

"Just let that be!" It was LeCroix's voice, from inside the *Pioneer*. Harriman waited and listened. "None of your business!" the pilot's voice went on, rising higher, "and put them back!"

Harriman pushed his way to the door of the ship. "What's the trouble, Les?"

Inside the cramped cabin, hardly large enough for a TV booth, three men stood—LeCroix and two reporters. All three men looked angry. "What's the trouble, Les?" Harriman repeated.

LeCroix was holding a small cloth bag which appeared to be empty. Scattered on the pilot's acceleration rest between him and the reporters were several small, dully brilliant stones. A reporter held one such stone up to the light.

"These guys were poking their noses into things that didn't concern them," LeCroix said angrily.

The reporter looked at the stone and said, "You told us to look at what we liked, didn't you, Mr. Harriman?"

"Yes."

"Your pilot here—" he jerked a thumb at LeCroix "—apparently didn't expect us to find these. He had them hidden in the pads of his chair."

"What of it?"

"They're diamonds."

"What makes you think so?"

"They're diamonds all right."

Harriman stopped and unwrapped a cigar. Presently he said, "Those diamonds were where you found them because I put them there."

A flashlight went off behind Harriman; a voice said, "Hold the rock up higher, Jeff."

The reporter called Jeff obliged, then said, "That seems an odd thing to do, Mr. Harriman."

"I was interested in the effect of outer space radiations on raw diamonds. On my orders Captain LeCroix placed that sack of diamonds in the ship."

Jeff whistled thoughtfully. "You know, Mr. Harriman, if you did not have that explanation, I'd think LeCroix had found the rocks on the Moon and was trying to hold out on you."

"Print that and you will be sued for libel. I have every confidence in Captain LeCroix. Now give me the diamonds."

Jeff's eyebrows went up. "But not confidence enough in him to let him keep them, maybe?"

"Give me the stones. Then get out."

Harriman got LeCroix away from the reporters as quickly as possible and into Harriman's own ship. "That's all for now," he told the news and pictures people. "See us at Peterson Field."

Once the ship raised ground he turned to LeCroix. "You did a beautiful job, Les."

"That reporter named Jeff must be sort of confused."

"Eh? Oh, *that*. No, I mean the flight. You did it. You're head man on this planet."

LeCroix shrugged it off. "Bob built a good ship. It was a cinch. Now about those diamonds—"

"Forget the diamonds. You've done your part. We placed those rocks in the ship; now we tell everybody we did—truthful as can be. It's not our fault if they don't believe us."

"But Mr. Harriman—"

"What?"

LeCroix unzipped a pocket in his coveralls, hauled out a soiled handkerchief, knotted into a bag. He untied it—and spilled into Harriman's hands many more diamonds than had been displayed in the ship—larger, finer diamonds.

Harriman stared at them. He began to chuckle.

Presently he shoved them back at LeCroix. "Keep them."

"I figure they belong to all of us."

."Well, keep them for us, then. And keep your mouth shut about them. No, wait." He picked out two large stones. "I'll have rings made from these two, one for you, one for me. But keep your mouth shut, or they won't be worth anything, except as curiosities."

It was quite true, he thought. Long ago the diamond syndicate had realized that diamonds in plentiful supply were worth little more than glass, except for industrial uses. Earth had more than enough for that, more than enough for jewels. If Moon diamonds were literally "common as pebbles" then they were just that—pebbles.

Not worth the expense of bringing them to earth.

But now take uranium. If that were plentiful—

Harriman sat back and indulged in daydreaming.

Presently LeCroix said softly, "You know, Boss, it's wonderful there."

"Eh? Where?"

"Why, on the Moon of course. I'm going back. I'm going back just as soon as I can. We've got to get busy on the new ship."

"Sure, sure! And this time we'll build one big enough for all of us. This time I go, too!"

"You bet."

"Les—" The older man spoke almost diffidently. "What does it look like when you look back and see the Earth?"

"Huh? It looks like—It looks—" LeCroix stopped. "Hell's bells, Boss, there isn't any way to tell you. It's wonderful, that's all. The sky is black and—well, wait until you see the pictures I took. Better yet, wait and see it yourself."

Harriman nodded. "But it's hard to wait."

11

FIELDS OF DIAMONDS ON THE MOON!!!
BILLIONAIRE BACKER DENIES DIAMOND STORY

Says Jewels Taken into Space for Science Reasons
      MOON DIAMONDS: HOAX OR FACT?

—but consider this, friends of the invisible audience: why would anyone take diamonds *to* the moon? Every ounce of that ship and its cargo was calculated; diamonds would not be taken along without reason. Many scientific authorities have pronounced Mr. Harriman's professed reason an absurdity. It is easy to guess that diamonds might be taken along for the purpose of "salting" the Moon, so to speak, with earthly jewels, with the intention of convincing us that diamonds exist on the Moon—but Mr. Harriman, his pilot Captain LeCroix, and everyone connected with the enterprise have sworn from the beginning that the diamonds *did not* come from the Moon. But it is an absolute certainty that the diamonds were in the space ship when it landed. Cut it how you will; this reporter is going to try to buy some lunar diamond mining stock—

Strong was, as usual, already in the office when Harriman came in. Before the partners could speak, the screen called out, "Mr. Harriman, Rotterdam calling."

"Tell them to go plant a tulip."

"Mr. van der Velde is waiting, Mr. Harriman."

"Okay."

Harriman let the Hollander talk, then said, "Mr. van der Velde, the statements attributed to me are absolutely correct. I put those diamonds the reporters saw into the ship before it took off. They were mined right here on Earth. In fact I bought them when I came over to see you; I can prove it."

"But Mr. Harriman—"

"Suit yourself. There may be more diamonds on the Moon than you can run and jump over. I don't guarantee it. But I do guarantee that those diamonds the newspapers are talking about came from Earth."

"Mr. Harriman, why would you send diamonds to the Moon? Perhaps you intended to fool us, no?"

"Have it your own way. But I've said all along that those diamonds came from Earth. Now see here: you took an option—an option on an option, so to speak. If you want to make the second payment on that option and keep it in force, the deadline is nine o'clock Thursday, New York time, as specified in the contract. Make up your mind."

He switched off and found his partner looking at him sourly. "What's eating you?"

"I wondered about those diamonds, too, Delos. So I've been looking through the weight schedule of the *Pioneer*."

"Didn't know you were interested in engineering."

"I can read figures."

"Well, you found it, didn't you? Schedule F-17-c, two ounces, allocated to me personally."

"I found it. It sticks out like a sore thumb. But I didn't find something else."

Harriman felt a cold chill in his stomach. "What?"

"I didn't find a schedule for the canceled covers." Strong stared at him.

"It must be there. Let me see that weight schedule."

"It's not there, Delos. You know, I thought it was funny when you insisted on going to meet Captain LeCroix by yourself. What happened, Delos? Did you sneak them aboard?" He continued to stare while Harriman fidgeted. "We've put over some sharp business deals—but this will be the first time that anyone can say that the firm of Harriman and Strong has cheated."

"Damn it, George—I would cheat, lie, steal, beg, bribe—do *anything* to accomplish what we have accomplished."

Harriman got up and paced the room. "We *had* to have that money, or the ship would never have taken off. We're cleaned out. You know that, don't you?"

Strong nodded. "But those covers should have gone to the Moon. That's what we contracted to do."

"Damn it, I just forgot it. Then it was too late to figure the weight in. But it doesn't matter. I figured that if the trip was a failure, if LeCroix cracked up, nobody would know or care that the covers hadn't gone. And I knew if he made it, it wouldn't matter; we'd have plenty of money. And we will, George, we will!"

"We've got to pay the money back."

"Now? Give me time, George. Everybody concerned is happy the way it is. Wait until we recover our stake; then I'll buy every one of those covers back—out of my own pocket. That's a promise."

Strong continued to sit. Harriman stopped in front of him. "I ask you, George, is it worthwhile to wreck an enterprise of this size for a purely theoretical point?"

Strong sighed and said, "When the time comes, use the firm's money."

"That's the spirit! But I'll use my own, I promise you."

"No, the firm's money. If we're in it together, we're in it together."

"Okay, if that's the way you want it."

Harriman turned back to his desk. Neither of the two partners had anything to say for a long while. Presently Dixon and Entenza were announced.

"Well, Jack," said Harriman. "Feel better now?"

"No thanks to you. I had to fight for what I did put on the air—and some of it was pirated as it was. Delos, there should have been a television pickup in the ship."

"Don't fret about it. As I told you, we couldn't spare the weight this time. But there will be the next trip, and the next. Your concession is going to be worth a pile of money."

Dixon cleared his throat. "That's what we came to see you about, Delos. What are your plans?"

"Plans? We go right ahead. Les and Coster and I make the next trip. We set up a permanent base. Maybe Coster stays behind. The third trip we send a real colony—nuclear engineers, miners, hydroponics experts, communications engineers. We'll found Luna City, first city on another planet."

Dixon looked thoughtful. "And when does this begin to pay off?"

"What do you mean by 'pay off'? Do you want your capital back, or do you want to begin to see some return on your investment? I can cut it either way."

Entenza was about to say that he wanted his investment back; Dixon cut in first. "Profits, naturally. The investment is already made."

"Fine!"

"But I don't see how you expect profits. Certainly, LeCroix made the trip and got back safely. There is honor for all of us. But where are the royalties?"

"Give the crop time to ripen, Dan. Do I look worried? What are our assets?" Harriman ticked them off on his fingers. "Royalties on pictures, television, radio—"

"Those things go to Jack."

"Take a look at the agreement. He has the concession, but he pays the firm—that's all of us—for them."

Dixon said, "Shut up, Jack!" before Entenza could speak, then added, "What else? That won't pull us out of the red."

"Endorsements galore. Monty's boys are working on that. Royalties from the greatest best seller yet—I've got a ghost-writer and a stenographer following LeCroix around this very minute. A franchise for the first and only space line—"

"From whom?"

"We'll get it. Kamens and Montgomery are in Paris now, working on it. I'm joining them this afternoon. And we'll tie down that franchise with a franchise from *the other end,* just as soon as we can get a permanent colony there, no matter how small. It will be the autonomous state of Luna, under the protection of the United Nations—and no ship will land or take off in its territory without its permission. Besides that we'll have the right to franchise a dozen other companies for various purposes—and tax them, too—just as soon as we set up the Municipal Corporation of the City of Luna under the laws of the

State of Luna. We'll sell everything but vacuum—we'll even sell vacuum, for experimental purposes. And don't forget—we'll still have a big chunk of real estate, sovereign title in us—as a state—and not yet sold. The Moon is *big*."

"Your ideas are rather big, too, Delos," Dixon said dryly. "But what actually happens next?"

"First we get title confirmed by the UN. The Security Council is now in secret session; the Assembly meets tonight. Things will be popping; that's why I've got to be there. When the United Nations decides—as it will—that its own nonprofit corporation has the only real claim to the Moon, then I get busy. The poor little weak nonprofit corporation is going to grant a number of things to some real honest-to-God corporations with hair on their chests—in return for help in setting up a physics research lab, an astronomical observatory, a lunography institute and some other perfectly proper nonprofit enterprises. That's our interim pitch until we get a permanent colony with its own laws. Then we—"

Dixon gestured impatiently. "Never mind the legal shenanigans, Delos. I've known you long enough to know that you can figure out such angles. What do we actually have to *do* next?"

"Huh? We've got to build another ship, a bigger one. Not actually bigger, but effectively bigger. Coster has started the design of a surface catapult—it will reach from Manitou Springs to the top of Pikes Peak. With it we can put a ship in free orbit around the Earth. Then we'll use such a ship to fuel more ships —it amounts to a space station, like the power station. It adds up to a way to get there on chemical power without having to throw away nine-tenths of your ship to do it."

"Sounds expensive."

"It will be. But don't worry; we've got a couple of dozen piddling little things to keep the money coming in while we get set up on a commercial basis, then we sell stock. We sold stock before; now we'll sell a thousand dollars' worth where we sold ten before."

"And you think that will carry you through until the enterprise as a whole is on a paying basis? Face it, Delos, the thing as a whole doesn't pay off until you have ships plying between here and the Moon on a paying basis, figured in freight and passenger charges. That means customers, with cash. What is there on the Moon to ship—and who pays for it?"

"Dan, don't you believe there will be? If not, why are you here?"

"I believe in it, Delos—or I believe in you. But what's your time schedule? What's your budget? What's your prospective commodity? And please don't mention diamonds; I think I understand that caper."

Harriman chewed his cigar for a few moments. "There's one valuable commodity we'll start shipping at once."

"What?"

"Knowledge."

Entenza snorted. Strong looked puzzled. Dixon nodded. "I'll buy that. Knowledge is always worth something—to the man who knows how to exploit it. And I'll agree that the Moon is a place to find new knowledge. I'll assume that you can make the next trip pay off. What's your budget and your timetable for that?"

Harriman did not answer. Strong searched his face closely. To him Harriman's poker face was as revealing as large print—he decided that his partner had been crowded into a corner. He waited, nervous but ready to back Harriman's play.

Dixon went on. "From the way you describe it, Delos, I judge that you don't have money enough for your next step—and you don't know where you will get it. I believe in you, Delos—and I told you at the start that I did not believe in letting a new business die of anemia. I'm ready to buy in with a fifth share."

Harriman stared. "Look," he said bluntly, "you own Jack's share now, don't you?"

"I wouldn't say that."

"You vote it. It sticks out all over."

Entenza said, "That's not true. I'm independent. I—"

"Jack, you're a damn liar," Harriman said dispassionately. "Dan, you've got fifty percent now. Under the present rules I decide deadlocks, which gives me control as long as George sticks by me. If we sell you another share, you vote three-fifths —and are boss. Is that the deal you are looking for?"

"Delos, as I told you, I have confidence in you."

"But you'd feel happier with the whip hand. Well, I won't do it. I'll let space travel—*real* space travel, with established runs —wait another twenty years before I'll turn loose. I'll let us all go broke and let us live on glory before I'll turn loose. You'll have to think up another scheme."

Dixon said nothing. Harriman got up and began to pace. He stopped in front of Dixon. "Dan, if you really understood what this is all about, I'd let you have control. But you don't. You see this as just another way to money and to power. I'm perfectly willing to let you vultures get rich—but I keep control. I'm going to see this thing developed, not milked. The human race is heading out to the stars—and this adventure is going to present new problems compared with which atomic power was a kid's toy. The race is about as prepared for it as an innocent virgin is prepared for sex. Unless the whole matter is handled carefully, it will be bitched up. *You'll* bitch it up, Dan, if I let you have the deciding vote in it—because you don't understand it."

He caught his breath and went on, "Take safety for instance. Do you know *why* I let LeCroix take that ship out instead of taking it myself? Do you think I was afraid? No! I wanted it to come back—*safely*. I didn't want space travel getting another setback. Do you know why we have to have a monopoly, for a few years at least? Because every so-and-so and his brother is going to want to build a Moon ship, now that they know it can be done. Remember the first days of ocean flying? After Lindbergh did it, every so-called pilot who could lay hands on a crate took off for some over-water point. Some of them even took their kids along. And most of them landed in the drink. Airplanes got a reputation for being dangerous. A few years after that the airlines got so hungry for quick money in a highly competitive field that you couldn't pick up a paper without seeing headlines about another airliner crash.

"That's not going to happen to space travel! I'm not going to let it happen. Space ships are too big and too expensive; if they get a reputation for being unsafe as well, we might as well have stayed in bed. I run things."

He stopped. Dixon waited and then said, "I said I believed in you, Delos. How much money do you need?"

"Eh? On what terms?"

"Your note."

"My note? Did you say *my note?*"

"I'd want security, of course."

Harriman swore. "I knew there was a hitch in it. Dan, you know damn well everything I've got is tied up in this venture."

"You have insurance. You have quite a lot of insurance, I know."

"Yes, but that's all made out to my wife."

"I seem to have heard you say something about that sort of thing to Jack Entenza," Dixon said. "Come, now—if I know your tax-happy sort, you have at least one irrevocable trust, or paid-up annuities, or something, to keep Mrs. Harriman out of the poorhouse."

Harriman thought fiercely about it. "When's the call date on this note?"

"In the sweet bye and bye. I want a no-bankruptcy clause, of course."

"Why? Such a clause has no legal validity."

"It would be valid with *you*, wouldn't it?"

"Mmm . . . yes. Yes, it would."

"Then get out your policies and see how big a note you can write."

Harriman looked at him, turned abruptly and went to his safe. He came back with quite a stack of long, stiff folders. They added them up together; it was an amazingly large sum—for those days. Dixon then consulted a memorandum taken from his pocket and said, "One seems to be missing—a rather large one. A North Atlantic Mutual policy, I think."

Harriman glared at him. "Damn you, am I going to have to fire every confidential clerk in my force?"

"No," Dixon said mildly, "I don't get my information from your staff."

Harriman went back to the safe, got the policy and added it to the pile. Strong spoke up. "Do you want mine, Mr. Dixon?"

"No," answered Dixon, "that won't be necessary." He started stuffing the policies in his pocket. "I'll keep these, Delos, and attend to keeping up the premiums. I'll bill you of course. You can send the note and the change-of-beneficiary forms to my office. Here's your draft." He took out another slip of paper; it was the draft—already made out in the amount of the policies.

Harriman looked at it. "Sometimes," he said slowly, "I wonder who's kidding who?" He tossed the draft over to Strong. "Okay, George, take care of it. I'm off to Paris, boys. Wish me luck." He strode out as jauntily as a fox terrier.

Strong looked from the closed door to Dixon, then at the note. "I ought to tear this thing up!"

"Don't do it," advised Dixon. "You see, I really do believe in him." He added, "Ever read Carl Sandburg, George?"

"I'm not much of a reader."

"Try him sometime. He tells a story about a man who started a rumor that they had struck oil in Hell. Pretty soon everybody has left for Hell, to get in on the boom. The man who started the rumor watches them all go, then scratches his head and says to himself that there just *might* be something in it, after all. So he left for Hell, too."

Strong waited, finally said, "I don't get the point."

"The point is that I just want to be ready to protect myself if necessary, George—and so should you. Delos might begin believing his own rumors. Diamonds! Come, Jack."

12

The ensuing months were as busy as the period before the flight of the *Pioneer* (now honorably retired to the Smithsonian Institution). One engineering staff and great gangs of men were working on the catapult; two more staffs were busy with two new ships; the *Mayflower,* and the *Colonial;* a third ship was on the drafting tables. Ferguson was chief engineer for all of this; Coster, still buffered by Jock Berkeley, was engineering consultant, working where and as he chose. Colorado Springs was a boom town; the Denver-Trinidad roadcity settlements spread out at the Springs until they surrounded Peterson Field.

Harriman was as busy as a cat with two tails. The constantly expanding exploitation and promotion took eight full days a week of his time, but, by working Kamens and Montgomery almost to ulcers and by doing without sleep himself, he created frequent opportunities to run out to Colorado and talk things over with Coster.

Luna City, it was decided, would be founded on the very next trip. The *Mayflower* was planned for a payload not only of seven passengers, but with air, water and food to carry four of them over to the next trip; they would live in an aluminum Quonset-type hut, sealed, pressurized, and buried under the loose soil of Luna until—and assuming—they were succored.

The choice of the four extra passengers gave rise to another contest, another publicity exploitation—and more sale of stock. Harriman insisted that they be two married couples, over the united objections of scientific organizations everywhere. He gave in only to the extent of agreeing that there was no objection to all four being scientists, providing they constituted two married couples. This gave rise to several hasty marriages—and some divorces, after the choices were announced.

The *Mayflower* was the maximum size that calculations showed would be capable of getting into a free orbit around the Earth from the boost of the catapult, plus the blast of her own engines. Before she took off, four other ships, quite as large, would precede her. But they were not space ships; they were mere tankers—nameless. The most finicky of ballistic calculations, the most precise of launchings, would place them in the same orbit at the same spot. There the *Mayflower* would rendezvous and accept their remaining fuel.

This was the trickiest part of the entire project. If the four tankers could be placed close enough together, LeCroix, using a tiny maneuvering reserve, could bring his new ship to them. If not—well, it gets very lonely out in space.

Serious thought was given to placing pilots in the tankers and accepting as a penalty the use of enough fuel from one tanker to permit a getaway boat, a lifeboat with wings, to decelerate, reach the atmosphere and brake to a landing. Coster found a cheaper way.

A radar pilot, whose ancestor was the proximity fuse and whose immediate parents could be found in the homing devices of guided missiles, was given the task of bringing the tankers together. The first tanker would not be so equipped, but the second tanker through its robot would smell out the first and home on it with a pint-sized rocket engine, using the smallest of vectors to bring them together. The third would home on the first two and the fourth on the group.

LeCroix should have no trouble—if the scheme worked.

13

Strong wanted to show Harriman the sales reports on the H&S automatic household switch; Harriman brushed them aside.

Strong shoved them back under his nose. "You'd better start taking an interest in such things, Delos. *Somebody* around this office had better start seeing to it that some money comes in—some money that belongs to us, personally—or you'll be selling apples on a street corner."

Harriman leaned back and clasped his hands back of his head. "George, how can you talk that way on a day like this? Is there no poetry in your soul? Didn't you hear what I said when I came in? *The rendezvous worked.* Tankers one and two are as close together as Siamese twins. We'll be leaving within the week."

"That's as may be. Business has to go on."

"You keep it going; I've got a date. When did Dixon say he would be over?"

"He's due now."

"Good!" Harriman bit the end off a cigar and went on, "You know, George, I'm not sorry I didn't get to make the first trip. Now I've still got it to do. I'm as expectant as a bridegroom—and as happy." He started to hum.

Dixon came in without Entenza, a situation that had obtained since the day Dixon had dropped the pretense that he controlled only one share. He shook hands. "You heard the news, Dan?"

"George told me."

"This is it—or almost. A week from now, more or less, I'll be on the Moon. I can hardly believe it."

Dixon sat down silently. Harriman went on. "Aren't you even going to congratulate me? Man, this is a great day!"

Dixon said, "D. D., why are you going?"

"Huh? Don't ask foolish questions. This is what I have been working toward."

"It's not a foolish question. I asked why *you* were going. The four colonists have an obvious reason, and each is a selected specialist observer as well. LeCroix is the pilot. Coster is the man who is designing the permanent colony. But why are *you* going? What's your function?"

"My function? Why, I'm the guy who runs things. Shucks,

I'm going to run for mayor when I get there. Have a cigar, friend—the name's Harriman. Don't forget to vote." He grinned.

Dixon did not smile. "I did not know you planned on staying."

Harriman looked sheepish. "Well, that's still up in the air. If we get the shelter built in a hurry, we may save enough in the way of supplies to let me sort of lay over until the next trip. You wouldn't begrudge me that, would you?"

Dixon looked him in the eye. "Delos, I can't let you go at all."

Harriman was too startled to talk at first. At last he managed to say, "Don't joke, Dan. I'm going. You can't stop me. Nothing on Earth can stop me."

Dixon shook his head. "I can't permit it, Delos. I've got too much sunk in this. If you go and anything happens to you, I lose it all."

"That's silly. You and George would just carry on, that's all."

"Ask George."

Strong had nothing to say. He did not seem anxious to meet Harriman's eyes. Dixon went on. "Don't try to kid your way out of it, Delos. This venture is you and you are this venture. If you get killed, the whole thing folds up. I don't say space travel folds up; I think you've already given that a boost that will carry it along even with lesser men in your shoes. But as for this venture—our company—it will fold up. George and I will have to liquidate at about half a cent on the dollar. It would take sale of patent rights to get that much. The tangible assets aren't worth anything."

"Damn it, it's the intangibles we sell. You knew that all along."

"You are the intangible asset, Delos. You are the goose that lays the golden eggs. I want you to stick around until you've laid them. You must not risk your neck in space flight until you have this thing on a profit-making basis, so that any competent manager, such as George or myself, thereafter can keep it solvent. I mean it, Delos. I've got too much in it to see you risk it in a joyride."

Harriman stood up and pressed his fingers down on the edge of his desk. He was breathing hard. "You can't stop me!" he said slowly and forcefully. "You knew all along that I meant to go. You can't stop me now. Not all the forces of Heaven or Hell can stop me."

Dixon answered quietly, "I'm sorry, Delos. But I can stop you and I will. I can tie up that ship out there."

"Try it! I own as many lawyers as you do—and better ones!"

"I think you will find that you are not as popular in American courts as you once were—not since the United States found out it didn't own the Moon after all."

"Try it, I tell you. I'll break you and I'll take your shares away from you, too."

"Easy, Delos! I've no doubt you have some scheme whereby you could milk the basic company right away from George and me if you decided to. But it won't be necessary. Nor will it be necessary to tie up the ship. I want that flight to take place as much as you do. But you won't be on it, because you will decide not to go."

"I will, eh? Do I look crazy from where you sit?"

"No, on the contrary."

"Then why won't I go?"

"Because of your note that I hold. I want to collect it."

"What? There's no due date."

"No. But I want to be sure to collect it."

"Why, you dumb fool, if I get killed you collect it sooner than ever."

"Do I? You are mistaken, Delos. If you are killed—on a flight to the Moon—I collect nothing. I know; I've checked with every one of the companies underwriting you. Most of them have escape clauses covering experimental vehicles that date back to early aviation. In any case all of them will cancel and fight it out in court if you set foot inside that ship."

"You put them up to this!"

"Calm down, Delos. You'll be bursting a blood vessel. Certainly I queried them, but I was legitimately looking after my own interests. I don't want to collect on that note—not now, not by your death. I want you to pay it back out of your own earnings, by staying here and nursing this company through till it's stable."

Harriman chucked his cigar, almost unsmoked and badly chewed, at a wastebasket. He missed. "I don't give a hoot if you lose on it. If you hadn't stirred them up, they'd have paid without a quiver."

"But it did dig up a weak point in your plans, Delos. If space travel is to be a success, insurance will have to reach out and cover the insured anywhere."

"Damn it, one of them does now—N. A. Mutual."

"I've seen their ad and I've looked over what they claim to offer. It's just window dressing, with the usual escape clause. No, insurance will have to be revamped, all sorts of insurance."

Harriman looked thoughtful. "I'll look into it. George, call Kamens. Maybe we'll have to float our own company."

"Never mind Kamens," objected Dixon. "The point is you can't go on this trip. You have too many details of that sort to watch and plan for and nurse along."

Harriman looked back at him. "You haven't gotten it through your head, Dan, that *I'm going!* Tie up the ship if you can. If you put sheriffs around it, I'll have goons there to toss them aside."

Dixon looked pained. "I hate to mention this point, Delos, but I am afraid you will be stopped even if I drop dead."

"How?"

"Your wife."

"What's she got to do with it?"

"She's ready to sue for separate maintenance right now— she's found out about this insurance thing. When she hears about this present plan, she'll force you into court and force an accounting of your assets."

"You put her up to it!"

Dixon hesitated. He knew that Entenza had spilled the beans to Mrs. Harriman—maliciously. Yet there seemed no point in adding to a personal feud. "She's bright enough to have done some investigating on her own account. I won't deny I've talked to her—but she sent for me."

"I'll fight both of you!" Harriman stomped to a window, stood looking out—it was a real window; he liked to look at the sky.

Dixon came over and put a hand on his shoulder, saying softly, "Don't take it this way, Delos. Nobody's trying to keep you from your dream. But you can't go just yet; you can't let us down. We've stuck with you this far; you owe it to us to stick with us until it's done."

Harriman did not answer; Dixon went on. "If you don't feel any loyalty toward me, how about George? He's stuck with you *against* me, when it hurt him, when he thought you were ruining him—and you surely were, unless you finish this job. How about George, Delos? Are you going to let him down, too?"

Harriman swung around, ignoring Dixon and facing Strong. "What about it, George? Do you think I should stay behind?"

Strong rubbed his hands and chewed his lip. Finally he looked up. "It's all right with me, Delos. You do what you think is best."

Harriman stood looking at him for a long moment, his face working as if he were going to cry. Then he said huskily, "Okay, you bastards. Okay. I'll stay behind."

14

It was one of those glorious evenings so common in the Pikes Peak region, after a day in which the sky has been well scrubbed by thunderstorms. The track of the catapult crawled in a straight line up the face of the mountain, whole shoulders having been carved away to permit it. At the temporary spaceport, still raw from construction, Harriman, in company with visiting notables, was saying goodbye to the passengers and crew of the *Mayflower*.

The crowds came right up to the rail of the catapult. There was no need to keep them back from the ship; the jets would not blast until she was high over the peak. Only the ship itself was guarded, the ship and the gleaming rails.

Dixon and Strong, together for company and mutual support, hung back at the edge of the area roped off for passengers and officials. They watched Harriman jollying those about to leave: "Goodbye, Doctor. Keep an eye on him, Janet. Don't let him go looking for Moon Maidens." They saw him engage Coster in private conversation, then clap the younger man on the back.

"Keeps his chin up, doesn't he?" whispered Dixon.

"Maybe we should have let him go," answered Strong.

"Eh? Nonsense! We've got to have him. Anyway, his place in history is secure."

"He doesn't care about history," Strong answered seriously, "he just wants to go to the Moon."

"Well, confound it—he can go to the Moon . . . as soon as he gets his job done. After all, it's his job. He made it."

"I know."

Harriman turned around, saw them, started toward them. They shut up. "Don't duck," he said jovially. "It's all right. I'll go on the next trip. By then I plan to have it running itself. You'll see." He turned back toward the *Mayflower*. "Quite a sight, isn't she?"

The outer door was closed; ready lights winked along the track and from the control tower. A siren sounded.

Harriman moved a step or two closer.

"There she goes!"

It was a shout from the whole crowd. The great ship started

slowly, softly up the track, gathered speed, and shot toward the distant peak. She was already tiny by the time she curved up the face and burst into the sky.

She hung there a split second, then a plume of light exploded from her tail. Her jets had fired.

Then she was a shining light in the sky, a ball of flame, then —nothing. She was gone, upward and outward, to her rendezvous with her tankers.

The crowd had pushed to the west end of the platform as the ship swarmed up the mountain. Harriman had stayed where he was, nor had Dixon and Strong followed the crowd. The three were alone, Harriman most alone, for he did not seem aware that the others were near him. He was watching the sky.

Strong was watching him. Presently Strong barely whispered to Dixon, "Do you read the Bible?"

"Some."

"He looks as Moses must have looked, when he gazed out over the Promised Land."

Harriman dropped his eyes from the sky and saw them. "You guys still here?" he said. "Come on—there's work to be done."

The Marching Morons

The Marching Morons

C. M. KORNBLUTH

The late C. M. Kornbluth, who died when he was thirty-five, was one of the most prolific and talented writers this field has produced. In this story he examines a proposition that I believe in myself—that, all things considered, the Stupids are more dangerous than the Crazies.

Some things had not changed. A potter's wheel was still a potter's wheel and clay was still clay. Efim Hawkins had built his shop near Goose Lake, which had a narrow band of good fat clay and a narrow beach of white sand. He fired three bottle-nosed kilns with willow charcoal from the wood lot. The wood lot was also useful for long walks while the kilns were cooling; if he let himself stay within sight of them, he would open them prematurely, impatient to see how some new shape or glaze had come through the fire, and—*ping!*—the new shape or glaze would be good for nothing but the shard pile back of his slip tanks.

A business conference was in full swing in his shop, a modest cube of brick, tile-roofed, as the Chicago-Los Angeles "rocket" thundered overhead—very noisy, very swept back, very fiery jets, shaped as sleekly swift-looking as an airborne barracuda.

The buyer from Marshall Fields was turning over a black-glazed one-liter carafe, nodding approval with his massive, handsome head. "This is real pretty," he told Hawkins and his own

121

secretary, Gomez-Laplace. "This has got lots of what ya call real est'etic principles. Yeah, it is real pretty."

"How much?" the secretary asked the potter.

"Seven-fifty in dozen lots," said Hawkins. "I ran up fifteen dozen last month."

"They are real est'etic," repeated the buyer from Fields. "I will take them all."

"I don't think we can do that, doctor," said the secretary. "They'd cost us $1,350. That would leave only $532 in our quarter's budget. And we still have to run down to East Liverpool to pick up some cheap dinner sets."

"Dinner sets?" asked the buyer, his big face full of wonder.

"Dinner sets. The department's been out of them for two months now. Mr. Garvy-Seabright got pretty nasty about it yesterday. Remember?"

"Garvy-Seabright, that meat-headed bluenose," the buyer said contemptuously. "He don't know nothin' about est'etics. Why for don't he lemme run my own department?" His eye fell on a stray copy of *Whambozambo Comix* and he sat down with it. An occasional deep chuckle or grunt of surprise escaped him as he turned the pages.

Uninterrupted, the potter and the buyer's secretary quickly closed a deal for two dozen of the liter carafes. "I wish we could take more," said the secretary, "but you heard what I told him. We've had to turn away customers for ordinary dinnerware because he shot the last quarter's budget on some Mexican piggy banks some equally enthusiastic importer stuck him with. The fifth floor is packed solid with them."

"I'll bet they look mighty est'etic."

"They're painted with purple cacti."

The potter shuddered and caressed the glaze of the sample carafe.

The buyer looked up and rumbled, "Ain't you dummies through yakkin' yet? What good's a seckertary for if'n he don't take the burden of *de*-tail off'n my back, harh?"

"We're all through, doctor. Are you ready to go?"

The buyer grunted peevishly, dropped *Whambozambo Comix* on the floor and led the way out of the building and down the log corduroy road to the highway. His car was waiting on the concrete. It was, like all contemporary cars, too low slung to get over the logs. He climbed down into the car and started the motor with a tremendous sparkle and roar.

"Gomez-Laplace," called out the potter under cover of the noise, "did anything come of the radiation program they were working on the last time I was on duty at the Pole?"

"The same old fallacy," said the secretary gloomily. "It stopped us on mutation, it stopped us on culling, it stopped us on segregation, and now it's stopped us on hypnosis."

"Well, I'm scheduled back to the grind in nine days. Time for another firing right now. I've got a new luster to try . . ."

"I'll miss you. I shall be 'vacationing'—running the drafting room of the New Century Engineering Corporation in Denver. They're going to put up a two-hundred-story office building, and naturally somebody's got to be on hand."

"Naturally," said Hawkins with a sour smile.

There was an ear-piercingly sweet blast as the buyer leaned on the horn button. Also, a yard-tall jet of what looked like flame spurted up from the car's radiator cap; the car's power plant was a gas turbine and had no radiator.

"I'm coming, doctor," said the secretary dispiritedly. He climbed down into the car and it whooshed off with much flame and noise.

The potter, depressed, wandered back up the corduroy road and contemplated his cooling kilns. The rustling wind in the boughs was obscuring the creak and mutter of the shrinking refractory brick. Hawkins wondered about the number two kiln—a reduction fire on a load of lusterware mugs. Had the clay chinking excluded the air? Had it been a properly smoky blaze? Would it do any harm if he just took one close—?

Common sense took Hawkins by the scruff of the neck and

yanked him over to the tool shed. He got out his pick and reso-
lutely set off on a prospecting jaunt to a hummocky field that
might yield some oxides. He was especially low on coppers.

The long walk left him sweating hard, with his lust for a peek
into the kiln quiet in his breast. He swung his pick almost at
random into one of the hummocks; it clanged on a stone which
he excavated. A largely obliterated inscription said:

ERSITY OF CHIC
OGICAL LABO
ELOVED MEMORY OF
KILLED IN ACT

The potter swore mildly. He had hoped the field would turn
out to be a cemetery, preferably a once-fashionable cemetery
full of once-massive bronze caskets moldered into oxides of tin
and copper.

Well, hell, maybe there was some around anyway.

He headed lackadaisically for the second largest hillock and
sliced into it with his pick. There was a stone to undercut and
topple into a trench, and then the potter was very glad he'd stuck
at it. His nostrils were filled with the bitter smell and the dirt
was tinged with the exciting blue of copper salts. The pick went
clang!

Hawkins, puffing, pried up a stainless steel plate that was
quite badly stained and was also marked with incised letters. It
seemed to have pulled loose from rotting bronze; there were
rivets on the back that brought up flakes of green patina. The
potter wiped off the surface dirt with his sleeve, turned it to
catch the sunlight obliquely and read:

HONEST JOHN BARLOW
Honest John, famed in university annals, represents a
challenge which medical science has not yet answered: re-

*vival of a human being accidentally thrown into a state of
suspended animation.*

*In 1988 Mr. Barlow, a leading Evanston real estate
dealer, visited his dentist for treatment of an impacted wis-
dom tooth. His dentist requested and received permission
to use the experimental anesthetic Cycloparadimethanol-
B-7, developed at the University.*

*After administration of the anesthetic, the dentist re-
sorted to his drill. By freakish mischance, a short circuit
in his machine delivered 220 volts of 60-cycle current into
the patient. (In a damage suit instituted by Mrs. Barlow
against the dentist, the University and the makers of the
drill, a jury found for the defendants.) Mr. Barlow never
got up from the dentist's chair and was assumed to have
died of poisoning, electrocution or both.*

*Morticians preparing him for embalming discovered,
however, that their subject was—though certainly not living—just as certainly not dead. The University was notified
and a series of exhaustive tests was begun, including
attempts to duplicate the trance state on volunteers. After
a bad run of seven cases which ended fatally, the attempts
were abandoned.*

*Honest John was long an exhibit at the University mu-
seum and livened many a football game as mascot of the
University's Blue Crushers. The bounds of taste were over-
stepped, however, when a pledge to Sigma Delta Chi was
ordered in '03 to "kidnap" Honest John from his loosely
guarded glass museum case and introduce him into the
Rachel Swanson Memorial Girls' Gymnasium shower room.*

*On May 22, 2003, the University Board of Regents is-
sued the following order: "By unanimous vote, it is directed
that the remains of Honest John Barlow be removed from
the University museum and conveyed to the University's
Lieutenant James Scott III Memorial Biological Labora-
tories and there be securely locked in a specially prepared*

vault. It is further directed that all possible measures for the preservation of these remains be taken by the Laboratory administration and that access to these remains be denied to all persons except qualified scholars authorized in writing by the Board. The Board reluctantly takes this action in view of recent notices and photographs in the nation's press which, to say the least, reflect but small credit upon the University."

It was far from his field, but Hawkins understood what had happened—an early and accidental blundering onto the bare bones of the Levantman shock anesthesia, which had since been replaced by other methods. To bring subjects out of Levantman shock, you let them have a squirt of simple saline in the trigeminal nerve. Interesting. And now about that bronze—

He heaved the pick into the rotting green salts, expecting no resistance, and almost fractured his wrist. *Something* down there was *solid*. He began to flake off the oxides.

A half hour of work brought him down to phosphor bronze, a huge casting of the almost incorruptible metal. It had weakened structurally over the centuries; he could fit the point of his pick under a corroded boss and pry off great creaking and grumbling striae of the stuff.

Hawkins wished he had an archaeologist with him but didn't dream of returning to his shop and calling one to take over the find. He was an all-around man: by choice, and in his free time an artist in clay and glaze; by necessity, an automotive, electronics and atomic engineer who could also swing a project in traffic control, individual and group psychology, architecture or tool design. He didn't yell for a specialist every time something out of his line came up; there were so few with so much to do . . .

He trenched around his find, discovering that it was a great brick-shaped bronze mass with an excitingly hollow sound. A long strip of moldering metal from one of the long vertical faces pulled away, exposing red rust that went *whoosh* and was sucked into the interior of the mass.

It had been de-aired, thought Hawkins, and there must have been an inner jacket of glass which had crystallized through the centuries and quietly crumbled at the first clang of his pick. He didn't know what a vacuum would do to a subject of Levantman shock, but he had hopes, nor did he quite understand what a real estate dealer was, but it might have something to do with pottery. And *anything* might have a bearing on Topic Number One.

He flung his pick out of the trench, climbed out and set off at a dog-trot for his shop. A little rummaging turned up a hypo and there was a plastic container of salt in the kitchen.

Back at his dig, he chipped for another half hour to expose the juncture of lid and body. The hinges were hopeless; he smashed them off.

Hawkins extended the telescopic handle of the pick for the best leverage, fitted its point into a deep pit, set its built-in fulcrum, and heaved. Five more heaves and he could see, inside the vault, what looked like a dusty marble statue. Ten more and he could see that it was the naked body of Honest John Barlow, Evanston real estate dealer, uncorrupted by time.

The potter found the apex of the trigeminal nerve with his needle's point and gave him 60 cc.

In an hour Barlow's chest began to pump.

In another hour, he rasped, "Did it work?"

"*Did* it!" muttered Hawkins.

Barlow opened his eyes and stirred, looked down, turned his hands before his eyes—

"I'll sue!" he screamed. "My clothes! My fingernails!" A horrid suspicion came over his face and he clapped his hands to his hairless scalp. "My hair!" he wailed. "I'll sue you for every penny you've got! That release won't mean a damned thing in court—I didn't sign away my hair and clothes and fingernails!"

"They'll grow back," said Hawkins casually. "Also your epidermis. Those parts of you weren't alive, you know, so they weren't preserved like the rest of you. I'm afraid the clothes are gone, though."

"What is this—the University hospital?" demanded Barlow. "I want a phone. No, you phone. Tell my wife I'm all right and tell Sam Immerman—he's my lawyer—to get over here right away. Greenleaf 7-4022. Ow!" He had tried to sit up, and a portion of his pink skin rubbed against the inner surface of the casket, which was powdered by the ancient crystallized glass. "What the hell did you guys do, boil me alive? Oh, you're going to pay for this!"

"You're all right," said Hawkins, wishing now he had a reference book to clear up several obscure terms. "Your epidermis will start growing immediately. You're not in the hospital. Look here."

He handed Barlow the stainless steel plate that had labeled the casket. After a suspicious glance, the man started to read. Finishing, he laid the plate carefully on the edge of the vault and was silent for a spell.

"Poor Verna," he said at last. "It doesn't say whether she was stuck with the court costs. Do you happen to know—"

"No," said the potter. "All I know is what was on the plate, and how to revive you. The dentist accidentally gave you a dose of what we call Levantman shock anesthesia. We haven't used it for centuries; it was powerful, but too dangerous."

"Centuries . . ." brooded the man. "Centuries . . . I'll bet Sam swindled her out of her eyeteeth. Poor Verna. How long ago was it? What year is this?"

Hawkins shrugged. "We call it 7-B-936. That's no help to you. It takes a long time for these metals to oxidize."

"Like that movie," Barlow muttered. "Who would have thought it? Poor Verna!" He blubbered and sniffled, reminding Hawkins powerfully of the fact that he had been found under a flat rock.

Almost angrily, the potter demanded, "How many children did you have?"

"None yet," sniffed Barlow. "My first wife didn't want them. But Verna wants one—wanted one—but we're going to wait until—we *were* going to wait until—"

"Of course," said the potter, feeling a savage desire to tell him off, blast him to hell and gone for his work. But he choked it down. There was The Problem to think of; there was always The Problem to think of, and this poor blubberer might unexpectedly supply a clue. Hawkins would have to pass him on.

"Come along," Hawkins said. "My time is short."

Barlow looked up, outraged. "How can you be so unfeeling? I'm a human being like—"

The Los Angeles-Chicago "rocket" thundered overhead and Barlow broke off in mid-complaint. "Beautiful!" he breathed, following it with his eyes. "Beautiful!"

He climbed out of the vault, too interested to be pained by its roughness against his infantile skin. "After all," he said briskly, "this should have its sunny side. I never was much for reading, but this is just like one of those stories. And I ought to make some money out of it, shouldn't I?" He gave Hawkins a shrewd glance.

"You want money?" asked the potter. "Here." He handed over a fistful of change and bills. "You'd better put my shoes on. It'll be about a quarter mile. Oh, and you're—uh, modest?—yes, that was the word. Here." Hawkins gave him his pants, but Barlow was excitedly counting the money.

"Eighty-five, eighty-six—and it's dollars, too! I thought it'd be credits or whatever they call them. 'E Pluribus Unum' and 'Liberty'—just different faces. Say, is there a catch to this? Are these real, genuine, honest twenty-two-cent dollars like we had or just wallpaper?"

"They're quite all right, I assure you," said the potter. "I wish you'd come along. I'm in a hurry."

The man babbled as they stumped toward the shop. "Where

are we going—The Council of Scientists, the World Coordinato
or something like that?"

"Who? Oh, no. We call them 'President' and 'Congress.' No
that wouldn't do any good at all. I'm just taking you to see som
people."

"I ought to make plenty out of this. *Plenty!* I could writ
books. Get some smart young fellow to put it into words for m
and I'll bet I could turn out a best seller. What's the setup or
things like that?"

"It's about like that. Smart young fellows. But there aren't an
best sellers any more. People don't read much nowadays. We'l
find something equally profitable for you to do."

Back in the shop, Hawkins gave Barlow a suit of clothes, de
posited him in the waiting room and called Central in Chicago
"Take him away," he pleaded. "I have time for one more firing
and he blathers and blathers. I haven't told him anything. Per
haps we should just turn him loose and let him find his own
level, but there's a chance—"

"The Problem," agreed Central. "Yes, there's a chance."

The potter delighted Barlow by making him a cup of coffee
with a cube that not only dissolved in cold water but heated the
water to boiling point. Killing time, Hawkins chatted about the
"rocket" Barlow had admired and had to haul himself up short
he had almost told the real estate man what its top speed really
was—almost, indeed, revealed that it was not a rocket.

He regretted, too, that he had so casually handed Barlow a
couple of hundred dollars. The man seemed obsessed with fear
that they were worthless since Hawkins refused to take a note or
I.O.U. or even a definite promise of repayment. But Hawkins
couldn't go into details, and was very glad when a stranger arrived from Central.

"Tinny-Peete, from Algeciras," the stranger told him swiftly
as the two of them met at the door. "Psychist for Poprob. Pol-
assigned special overtake Barlow."

"Thank Heaven," said Hawkins. "Barlow," he told the man

from the past, "this is Tinny-Peete. He's going to take care of you and help you make lots of money."

The psychist stayed for a cup of the coffee whose preparation had delighted Barlow, and then conducted the real estate man down the corduroy road to his car, leaving the potter to speculate on whether he could at last crack his kilns.

Hawkins, abruptly dismissing Barlow and the Problem, happily picked the chinking from around the door of the number two kiln, prying it open a trifle. A blast of heat and the heady, smoky scent of the reduction fire delighted him. He peered and saw a corner of a shelf glowing cherry red, becoming obscured by wavering black areas as it lost heat through the opened door. He slipped a charred wood paddle under a mug on the shelf and pulled it out as a sample, the hairs on the back of his hand curling and scorching. The mug crackled and pinged and Hawkins sighed happily.

The bismuth resinate luster had fired to perfection, a haunting film of silvery-black metal with strange bluish lights in it as it turned before the eyes, and the Problem of Population seemed very far away to Hawkins then.

Barlow and Tinny-Peete arrived at the concrete highway where the psychist's car was parked in a safety bay.

"What—a—*boat!*" gasped the man from the past.

"Boat? No, that's my car."

Barlow surveyed it with awe. Swept-back lines, deep-drawn compound curves, kilograms of chrome. He ran his hands over the door—or was it the door?—in a futile search for a handle, and asked respectfully, "How fast does it go?"

The psychist gave him a keen look and said slowly, "Two hundred and fifty. You can tell by the speedometer."

"Wow! My old Chevvy could hit a hundred on a straightaway, but you're out of my class, mister!"

Tinny-Peete somehow got a huge, low door open and Barlow descended three steps into immense cushions, floundering over to the right. He was too fascinated to pay serious attention to his flayed dermis. The dashboard was a lovely wilderness of dials, plugs, indicators, lights, scales and switches.

The psychist climbed down into the driver's seat and did something with his feet. The motor started like lighting a blow-torch as big as a silo. Wallowing around in the cushions, Barlow saw through a rear-view mirror a tremendous exhaust filled with brilliant white sparkles.

"Do you like it?" yelled the psychist.

"It's terrific!" Barlow yelled back. "It's—"

He was shut up as the car pulled out from the bay into the road with a great *voo-ooo-ooom!* A gale roared past Barlow's head, though the windows seemed to be closed; the impression of speed was terrific. He located the speedometer on the dashboard and saw it climb past 90, 100, 150, 200.

"Fast enough for me," yelled the psychist, noting that Barlow's face fell in response. "Radio?"

He passed over a surprisingly light object like a football helmet, with no trailing wires, and pointed to a row of buttons. Barlow put on the helmet, glad to have the roar of air stilled, and pushed a pushbutton. It lit up satisfyingly, and Barlow settled back even farther for a sample of the brave new world's supermodern taste in ingenious entertainment.

"TAKE IT AND STICK IT!" a voice roared in his ears.

He snatched off the helmet and gave the psychist an injured look. Tinny-Peete grinned and turned a dial associated with the pushbutton layout. The man from the past donned the helmet again and found the voice had lowered to normal.

"The show of shows! The supershow! The super-duper show! The quiz of quizzes! *Take It and Stick It!*"

There were shrieks of laughter in the background.

"Here we got the contes-tants all ready to go. You know how we work it. I hand a contes-tant a triangle-shaped cutout and like that down the line. Now we got these here boards, they got cutout places the same shape as the triangles and things, only they're all different shapes, and the first contes-tant that sticks the cutouts into the board, he wins.

"Now I'm gonna innaview the first contes-tant. Right here, honey. What's your name?"

"Name? Uh—"

"Hoddaya like that, folks? She don't remember her name! Hah? *Would you buy that for a quarter?*" The question was spoken with arch significance, and the audience shrieked, howled and whistled its appreciation.

It was dull listening when you didn't know the punch lines and catch lines. Barlow pushed another button, with his free hand ready at the volume control.

"—latest from Washington. It's about Senator Hull-Mendoza. He is still attacking the Bureau of Fisheries. The North California Syndicalist says he got affidavits that John Kingsley-Schultz is a bluenose from way back. He didn't publistat the affydavits, but he says they say that Kingsley-Schultz was saw at bluenose meetings in Oregon State College and later at Florida University. Kingsley-Schultz says he gotta confess he did major in fly casting at Oregon and got his Ph.D. in game-fish at Florida.

"And here is a quote from Kingsley-Schultz: 'Hull-Mendoza don't know what he's talking about. He should drop dead.' Unquote. Hull-Mendoza says he won't publistat the affydavits to pertect his sources. He says they was sworn by three former employes of the Bureau which was fired for in-competence and in-com-pat-ibility by Kingsley-Schultz.

"Elsewhere they was the usual run of traffic accidents. A three-way pileup of cars on Route 66 going outta Chicago took twelve lives. The Chicago-Los Angeles morning rocket crashed and exploded in the Mo-have—Mo-javvy—whatever-you-call-it Desert. All the 94 people aboard got killed. A Civil Aeronautics Authority investigator on the scene says that the pilot was buzzing herds of sheep and didn't pull out in time.

"Hey! Here's a hot one from New York! A diesel tug run wild in the harbor while the crew was below and shoved in the port bow of the luck-shury liner *S. S. Placentia*. It says the ship filled and sank taking the lives of an es-ti-mated 180 passengers and 50 crew members. Six divers was sent down to study the wreckage, but they died, too, when their suits turned out to be fulla little holes.

"And here is a bulletin I just got from Denver. It seems—"

Barlow took off the headset uncomprehendingly. "He seemed so callous," he yelled at the driver. "I was listening to a news-cast—"

Tinny-Peete shook his head and pointed at his ears. The roar of air was deafening. Barlow frowned baffledly and stared out of the window.

A glowing sign said:

MOOGS!
WOULD YOU BUY IT
FOR A QUARTER?

He didn't know what Moogs was or were; the illustration showed an incredibly proportioned girl, 99.9 percent naked, writhing passionately in animated full color.

The roadside jingle was still with him, but with a new feature. Radar or something spotted the car and alerted the lines of the jingle. Each in turn sped along a roadside track, even with the car, so it could be read before the next line was alerted.

IF THERE'S A GIRL
YOU WANT TO GET
DEFLOCCULIZE
UNROMANTIC SWEAT.
"A*R*M*P*I*T*T*O"

Another animated job, in two panels, the familiar "Before and After." The first said, "Just Any Cigar?" and was illustrated with a two-person domestic tragedy of a wife holding her nose while her coarse and red-faced husband puffed a slimy-looking rope. The second panel glowed, "Or a VUELTA ABAJO?" and was illustrated with—

Barlow blushed and looked at his feet until they had passed the sign.

"Coming into Chicago!" bawled Tinny-Peete.

Other cars were showing up, all of them dreamboats.

Watching them, Barlow began to wonder if he knew what a kilometer was, exactly. They seemed to be traveling so slowly, if you ignored the roaring air past your ears and didn't let the speedy lines of the dreamboats fool you. He would have sworn they were really crawling along at twenty-five, with occasional spurts up to thirty. How much was a kilometer, anyway?

The city loomed ahead, and it was just what it ought to be: towering skyscrapers, overhead ramps, landing platforms for helicopters—

He clutched at the cushions. Those two copters. They were going to—they were going to—they—

He didn't see what happened because their apparent collision courses took them behind a giant building.

Screamingly sweet blasts of sound surrounded them as they stopped for a red light. "What the hell is going on here?" said Barlow in a shrill, frightened voice, because the braking time was just about zero, and he wasn't hurled against the dashboard. "Who's kidding who?"

"Why, what's the matter?" demanded the driver.

The light changed to green and he started the pickup. Barlow stiffened as he realized that the rush of air past his ears began just a brief, unreal split second before the car was actually moving. He grabbed for the door handle on his side.

The city grew on them slowly: scattered buildings, denser buildings, taller buildings, and a red light ahead. The car rolled to a stop in zero braking time, the rush of air cut off an instant after it stopped, and Barlow was out of the car and running frenziedly down a sidewalk one instant after that.

They'll track me down, he thought, panting. *It's a secret police thing. They'll get you—mind-reading machines, television eyes everywhere, afraid you'll tell their slaves about freedom and stuff. They don't let anybody cross them, like that story I once read.*

Winded, he slowed to a walk and congratulated himself that he had guts enough not to turn around. That was what they always watched for. Walking, he was just another business-suited back among hundreds. He would be safe, he would be safe—

A hand gripped his shoulder and words tumbled from a large, coarse, handsome face thrust close to his: "Wassamatta bumpinninna people likeya owna sidewalk gotta miner slamya inna mushya bassar!" It was neither the mad potter nor the mad driver.

"Excuse me," said Barlow. "What did you say?"

"Oh, yeah?" yelled the stranger dangerously, and waited for an answer.

Barlow, with the feeling that he had somehow been suckered into the short end of an intricate land-title deal, heard himself reply belligerently, "Yeah!"

The stranger let go of his shoulder and snarled, "Oh, yeah?"

"Yeah!" said Barlow, yanking his jacket back into shape.

"Aaah!" snarled the stranger, with more contempt and disgust than ferocity. He added an obscenity current in Barlow's time, a standard but physiologically impossible directive, and strutted off hulking his shoulders and balling his fists.

Barlow walked on, trembling. Evidently he had handled it well enough. He stopped at a red light while the long, low dreamboats roared before him and pedestrians in the sidewalk flow with him threaded their ways through the stream of cars. Brakes screamed, fenders clanged and dented, hoarse cries flew back and forth between drivers and walkers. He leaped backward frantically as one car swerved over an arc of sidewalk to miss another.

The signal changed to green; the cars kept on coming for about thirty seconds and then dwindled to an occasional light runner. Barlow crossed warily and leaned against a vending machine, blowing big breaths.

Look natural, he told himself. *Do something normal. Buy something from the machine.* He fumbled out some change, got a newspaper for a dime, a handkerchief for a quarter and a candy bar for another quarter.

The faint chocolate smell made him ravenous suddenly. He clawed at the glassy wrapper printed *"Crigglies"* quite futilely for a few seconds, and then it divided neatly by itself. The bar made three good bites, and he bought two more and gobbled them down.

Thirsty, he drew a carbonated orange drink in another one of the glassy wrappers from the machine for another dime. When he fumbled with it, it divided neatly and spilled all over his knees. Barlow decided he had been there long enough and walked on.

The shop windows were—shop windows. People still wore and bought clothes, still smoked and bought tobacco, still ate and bought food. And they still went to the movies, he saw with pleased surprise as he passed and then returned to a glittering place whose sign said it was THE BIJOU.

The place seemed to be showing a triple feature, *Babies Are Terrible, Don't Have Children,* and *The Canali Kid.*

It was irresistible; he paid a dollar and went in.

He caught the tail end of *The Canali Kid* in three-dimensional, full-color, full-scent production. It appeared to be an interplanetary saga winding up with a chase scene and a reconciliation between estranged hero and heroine. *Babies Are Terrible* and *Don't Have Children* were fantastic arguments against parenthood—the grotesquely exaggerated dangers of painfully graphic childbirth, vicious children, old parents beaten and starved by their sadistic offspring. The audience, Barlow astoundedly noted, was placidly chomping sweets and showing no particular signs of revulsion.

The *Coming Attractions* drove him into the lobby. The fanfares were shattering, the blazing colors blinding, and the added scents stomach heaving.

When his eyes again became accustomed to the moderate lighting of the lobby, he groped his way to a bench and opened the newspaper he had bought. It turned out to be *The Racing Sheet,* which afflicted him with a crushing sense of loss. The familiar boxed index in the lower-left-hand corner of the front page showed almost unbearably that Churchill Downs and Empire City were still in business—

Blinking back tears, he turned to the Past Performance at Churchill. They weren't using abbreviations any more, and the pages because of that were single-column instead of double. But it was all the same—or was it?

He squinted at the first race, a three-quarter-mile maiden claimer for thirteen hundred dollars. Incredibly, the track record was two minutes, ten and three-fifths seconds. Any beetle in his time could have knocked off the three-quarter in one-fifteen. It was the same for the other distances, much worse for route events.

What the hell had happened to everything?

He studied the form of a five-year-old brown mare in the second and couldn't make head or tail of it. She'd won and lost and placed and showed and lost and placed without rhyme or reason. She looked like a front runner for a couple of races and then she looked like a no-good pig and then she looked like a mudder but the next time it rained she wasn't and then she was a stayer and then she was a pig again. In a good five-thousand-dollar allowances event, too!

Barlow looked at the other entries and it slowly dawned on him that they were all like the five-year-old brown mare. Not a single damned horse running had even the slightest trace of class.

Somebody sat down beside him and said, "That's the story."

Barlow whirled to his feet and saw it was Tinny-Peete, his driver.

"I was in doubts about telling you," said the psychist, "but I see you have some growing suspicions of the truth. Please don't get excited. It's all right, I tell you."

"So you've got me," said Barlow.

"Got you?"

"Don't pretend. I can put two and two together. You're the secret police. You and the rest of the aristocrats live in luxury on the sweat of these oppressed slaves. You're afraid of me because you have to keep them ignorant."

There was a bellow of bright laughter from the psychist that got them blank looks from other patrons of the lobby. The laughter didn't sound at all sinister.

"Let's get out of here," said Tinny-Peete, still chuckling. "You couldn't possibly have it more wrong." He engaged Barlow's arm and led him to the street. "The actual truth is that the millions of workers live in luxury on the sweat of the handful of aristocrats. I shall probably die before my time of overwork unless—" He gave Barlow a speculative look. "You may be able to help us."

"I know that gag," sneered Barlow. "I made money in my time and to make money you have to get people on your side. Go ahead and shoot me if you want, but you're not going to make a fool out of me."

"You nasty little ingrate!" snapped the psychist, with a kaleidoscopic change of mood. "This damned mess is all your fault and the fault of people like you! Now come along and no more of your nonsense."

He yanked Barlow into an office building lobby and an elevator that, disconcertingly, went *whoosh* loudly as it rose. The real estate man's knees were wobbly as the psychist pushed him from the elevator, down a corridor and into an office.

A hawk-faced man rose from a plain chair as the door closed

behind them. After an angry look at Barlow, he asked the psychist, "Was I called from the Pole to inspect this—this—?"

"Unget updandered. I've deeprobed etfind quasichance exhim Poprobattackline," said the psychist soothingly.

"Doubt," grunted the hawk-faced man.

"Try," suggested Tinny-Peete.

"Very well. Mr. Barlow, I understand you and your lamented had no children."

"What of it?"

"This of it. You were a blind, selfish stupid ass to tolerate economic and social conditions which penalized childbearing by the prudent and foresighted. You made us what we are today, and I want you to know that we are far from satisfied. Damnfool rockets! Damn-fool automobiles! Damn-fool cities with overhead ramps!"

"As far as I can see," said Barlow, "you're running down the best features of your time. Are you crazy?"

"The rockets aren't rockets. They're turbojets—good turbojets, but the fancy shell around them makes for a bad drag. The automobiles have a top speed of one hundred kilometers per hour—a kilometer is, if I recall my paleolinguistics, three-fifths of a mile—and the speedometers are all rigged accordingly so the drivers will think they're going two hundred and fifty. The cities are ridiculous, expensive, unsanitary, wasteful conglomerations of people who'd be better off and more productive if they were spread over the countryside.

"We need the rockets and trick speedometers and cities because, while you and your kind were being prudent and foresighted and not having children, the migrant workers, slum dwellers and tenant farmers were shiftlessly and shortsightedly having children—breeding, breeding. My God, how they bred!"

"Wait a minute," objected Barlow. "There were lots of people in our crowd who had two or three children."

"The attrition of accidents, illness, wars and such took care of that. Your intelligence was bred out. It is gone. Children that should have been born never were. The just-average, they'll-get-along majority took over the population. The average IQ now is 45."

"But that's far in the future—"

"So are you," grunted the hawk-faced man sourly.

"But who are *you* people?"

"Just people—real people. Some generations ago, the geneticists realized at last that nobody was going to pay any attention to what they said, so they abandoned words for deeds. Specifically, they formed and recruited for a closed corporation intended to maintain and improve the breed. We are their descendants, about three million of us. There are five billion of the others, so we are their slaves.

"During the past couple of years I've designed a skyscraper, kept Billings Memorial Hospital here in Chicago running, headed off war with Mexico and directed traffic at LaGuardia Field in New York."

"I don't understand! Why don't you let them go to hell in their own way?"

The man grimaced. "We tried it once for three months. We holed up at the South Pole and waited. They didn't notice it. Some drafting room people were missing, some chief nurses didn't show up, minor government people on the nonpolicy level couldn't be located. It didn't seem to matter.

"In a week there was hunger. In two weeks there were famine and plague, in three weeks war and anarchy. We called off the experiment; it took us most of the next generation to get things squared away again."

"But why *didn't* you let them kill each other off?"

"Five billion corpses mean about five hundred million tons of rotting flesh."

Barlow had another idea. "Why don't you sterilize them?"

"Two and one-half billion operations is a lot of operations. Because they breed continuously, the job would never be done."

"I see. Like the marching Chinese!"

"Who the devil are they?"

"It was a—uh—paradox of my time. Somebody figured out that if all the Chinese in the world were to line up four abreast, I think it was, and start marching past a given point, they'd never stop because of the babies that would be born and grow up before they passed the point."

"That's right. Only instead of 'a given point,' make it 'the largest conceivable number of operating rooms that we could build and staff.' There could never be enough."

"Say!" said Barlow. "Those movies about babies—was that your propaganda?"

"It was. It doesn't seem to mean a thing to them. We have abandoned the idea of attempting propaganda contrary to a biological drive."

"So if you work *with* a biological drive—?"

"I know of none which is consistent with inhibition of fertility."

Barlow's face went poker blank, the result of years of careful discipline. "You don't, huh? You're the great brains and you can't think of any?"

"Why, no," said the psychist innocently. "Can you?"

"That depends. I sold ten thousand acres of Siberian tundra—through a dummy firm, of course—after the partition of Russia. The buyers thought they were getting improved building lots on the outskirts of Kiev. I'd say that was a lot tougher than this job."

"How so?" asked the hawk-faced man.

"Those were normal, suspicious customers and these are morons, born suckers. You just figure out a con they'll fall for; they won't know enough to do any smart checking."

The psychist and the hawk-faced man had also had training; they kept themselves from looking with sudden hope at each other.

"You seem to have something in mind," said the psychist.

Barlow's poker face went blanker still. "Maybe I have. I haven't heard any offer yet."

"There's the satisfaction of knowing that you've prevented Earth's resources from being so plundered," the hawk-faced man pointed out, "that the race will soon become extinct."

"I don't know that," Barlow said bluntly. "All I have is your word."

"If you really have a method, I don't think any price would be too great," the psychist offered.

"Money," said Barlow.

"All you want."

"More than you want," the hawk-faced man corrected.

"Prestige," added Barlow. "Plenty of publicity. My picture and my name in the papers and over TV every day, statues to me, parks and cities and streets and other things named after me. A whole chapter in the history books."

The psychist made a facial sign to the hawk-faced man that meant, "Oh, brother!"

The hawk-faced man signaled back, "Steady, boy!"

"It's not too much to ask," the psychist agreed.

Barlow, sensing a seller's market, said, "Power!"

"Power?" the hawk-faced man repeated puzzledly. "Your own hydro station or nuclear pile?"

"I mean a world dictatorship with me as dictator!"

"Well, now—" said the psychist, but the hawk-faced man interrupted, "It would take a special emergency act of Congress but the situation warrants it. I think that can be guaranteed."

"Could you give us some indication of your plan?" the psychist asked.

"Ever hear of lemmings?"

"No."

"They are—were, I guess, since you haven't heard of them— little animals in Norway, and every few years they'd swarm to the coast and swim out to sea until they drowned. I figure on putting some lemming urge into the population."

"How?"

"I'll save that till I get the right signatures on the deal."

The hawk-faced man said, "I'd like to work with you on it, Barlow. My name's Ryan-Ngana." He put out his hand.

Barlow looked closely at the hand, then at the man's face. "Ryan what?"

"Ngana."

"That sounds like an African name."

"It is. My mother's father was a Watusi."

Barlow didn't take the hand. "I thought you looked pretty dark. I don't want to hurt your feelings, but I don't think I'd be at my best working with you. There must be somebody else just as well qualified, I'm sure."

The psychist made a facial sign to Ryan-Ngana that meant, "Steady *yourself*, boy!"

"Very well," Ryan-Ngana told Barlow. "We'll see what arrangement can be made."

"It's not that I'm prejudiced, you understand. Some of my best friends——"

"Mr. Barlow, don't give it another thought. Anybody who could pick on the lemming analogy is going to be useful to us."

And so he would, thought Ryan-Ngana, alone in the office after Tinny-Peete had taken Barlow up to the helicopter stage. So he would. Poprob had exhausted every rational attempt and the new Poprobattacklines would have to be irrational or subrational. This creature from the past with his lemming legends and his improved building lots would be a fountain of precious vicious self-interest.

Ryan-Ngana sighed and stretched. He had to go and run the San Francisco subway. Summoned early from the Pole to study Barlow, he'd left unfinished a nice little theorem. Between interruptions, he was slowly constructing an n-dimensional geometry whose foundations and superstructure owed no debt whatsoever to intuition.

Upstairs, waiting for a helicopter, Barlow was explaining to Tinny-Peete that he had nothing against Negroes, and Tinny-Peete wished he had some of Ryan-Ngana's imperturbability and humor for the ordeal.

The helicopter took them to International Airport where, Tinny-Peete explained, Barlow would leave for the Pole.

The man from the past wasn't sure he'd like a dreary waste of ice and cold.

"It's all right," said the psychist. "A civilized layout. Warm, pleasant. You'll be able to work more efficiently there. All the facts at your fingertips, a good secretary—"

"I'll need a pretty big staff," said Barlow, who had learned from thousands of deals never to take the first offer.

"I meant a private, confidential one," said Tinny-Peete readily, "but you can have as many as you want. You'll naturally have top-primary-top priority if you really have a workable plan."

"Let's not forget this dictatorship angle," said Barlow.

He didn't know that the psychist would just as readily have promised him deification to get him happily on the "rocket" for the Pole. Tinny-Peete had no wish to be torn limb from limb; he knew very well that it would end that way if the population learned from this anachronism that there was a small elite which considered itself head, shoulders, trunk and groin above the rest. The fact that this assumption was perfectly true and the fact that the elite was condemned by its superiority to a life of the most grinding toil would not be considered; the difference would.

The psychist finally put Barlow aboard the "rocket" with some thirty people—real people—headed for the Pole.

Barlow was airsick all the way because of a posthypnotic suggestion Tinny-Peete had planted in him. One idea was to make him as averse as possible to a return trip, and another idea was to spare the other passengers from his aggressive, talkative company.

Barlow during the first day at the Pole was reminded of his first day in the Army. It was the same now-where-the-hell-are-

we-going-to-put-*you?* business until he took a firm line with
them. Then instead of acting like supply sergeants they acted
like hotel clerks.

It was a wonderful, wonderfully calculated buildup, and one
that he failed to suspect. After all, in his time a visitor from the
past would have been lionized.

At day's end he reclined in a snug underground billet with the
sixty-mile gales roaring yards overhead and tried to put two and
two together.

It was like old times, he thought—like a coup in real estate
where you had the competition by the throat, like a fifty-percent
rent boost when you knew damned well there was no place for
the tenants to move, like smiling when you read over the breakfast orange juice that the city council had decided to build a
school on the ground you had acquired by a deal with the city
council. And it was simple. He would just sell tundra building
lots to eagerly suicidal lemmings, and that was absolutely all
there was to solving The Problem that had these double-domes
spinning.

They'd have to work out most of the details, naturally, but
what the hell, that was what subordinates were for. He'd need
specialists in advertising, engineering, communications—did
they know anything about hypnotism? That might be helpful. If
not, there'd have to be a lot of bribery done, but he'd make sure
—damned sure—there were unlimited funds.

Just selling building lots to lemmings . . .

He wished, as he fell asleep, that poor Verna could have been
in on this. It was his biggest, most stupendous deal. Verna—that
sharp shyster Sam Immerman must have swindled her . . .

It began the next day with people coming to visit him. He
knew the approach. They merely wanted to be helpful to their
illustrious visitor from the past and would he help fill them in
about his era, which unfortunately was somewhat obscure his-
torically, and what did he think could be done about The Prob-

lem? He told them he was too old to be roped any more, and they wouldn't get any information out of him until he got a letter of intent from at least the Polar President and a session of the Polar Congress empowered to make him dictator.

He got the letter and the session. He presented his program, was asked whether his conscience didn't revolt at its callousness, explained succinctly that a deal was a deal and anybody who wasn't smart enough to protect himself didn't deserve protection —"Caveat emptor," he threw in for scholarship, and had to translate it to "Let the buyer beware." He didn't, he stated, give a damn about either the morons or their intelligent slaves; he'd told them his price and that was all he was interested in.

Would they meet it or wouldn't they?

The Polar President offered to resign in his favor, with certain temporary emergency powers that the Polar Congress would vote him if he thought them necessary. Barlow demanded the title of World Dictator, complete control of world finances, salary to be decided by himself, and the publicity campaign and historical writeup to begin at once.

"As for the emergency powers," he added, "they are neither to be temporary nor limited."

Somebody wanted the floor to discuss the matter, with the declared hope that perhaps Barlow would modify his demands.

"You've got the proposition," Barlow said: "I'm not knocking off even ten percent."

"But what if the Congress refuses, sir?" the President asked.

"Then you can stay up here at the Pole and try to work it out yourselves. I'll get what I want from the morons. A shrewd operator like me doesn't have to compromise; I haven't got a single competitor in this whole cockeyed moronic era."

Congress waived debate and voted by show of hands. Barlow won unanimously.

"You don't know how close you came to losing me," he said in his first official address to the joint Houses. "I'm not the boy to haggle; either I get what I ask, or I go elsewhere. The first thing I want is to see designs for a new palace for me—nothing *unostentatious*, either—and your best painters and sculptors to start working on my portraits and statues. Meanwhile, I'll get my staff together."

He dismissed the Polar President and the Polar Congress, telling them that he'd let them know when the next meeting would be.

A week later, the program started with North America the first target.

Mrs. Garvy was resting after dinner before the ordeal of turning on the dishwasher. The TV, of course, was on and it said, "Oooh!"—long, shuddery and ecstatic, the cue for the *Parfum Assault Criminale* spot commercial. "Girls," said the announcer hoarsely, "do you want your man? It's easy to get him—easy as a trip to Venus."

"Huh?" said Mrs. Garvy.

"Wassamatter?" snorted her husband, starting out of a doze. "Ja hear that?"

"Wha'?"

"He said 'easy like a trip to Venus.' "

"So?"

"Well, I thought ya couldn't get to Venus. I thought they just had that one rocket thing that crashed on the Moon."

"Aah, women don't keep up with the news," said Garvy righteously, subsiding again.

"Oh," said his wife uncertainly.

And the next day, on *Henry's Other Mistress*, there was a new character who had just breezed in: Buzz Rentshaw, Master Rocket Pilot of the Venus run. On *Henry's Other Mistress*, "the broadcast drama about you and your neighbors, *folksy* people, *ordinary* people, *real* people!" Mrs. Garvy listened with amazement over a cooling cup of coffee as Buzz made hay of her hazy convictions.

MONA: Darling, it's so good to see you again!

BUZZ: You don't know how I've missed you on that dreary Venus run.

SOUND: *Venetian blind run down, key turned in lock.*

MONA: Was it *very* dull, dearest?

BUZZ: Let's not talk about my humdrum job, darling. Let's talk about us.

SOUND: *Creaking bed.*

Well, the program was back to normal at last. That evening Mrs. Garvy tried to ask again whether her husband was sure about those rockets, but he was dozing right through *Take It and Stick It*, so she watched the screen and forgot the puzzle.

She was still rocking with laughter at the gag line, "Would you buy it for a quarter?" when the commercial went on for the detergent powder she always faithfully loaded her dishwasher with on the first of every month.

The announcer displayed mountains of suds from a tiny piece of the stuff and coyly added, "Of course, Cleano don't lay around for you to pick up like the soap root on Venus, but it's pretty cheap and it's almost pretty near just as good. So for us plain folks who ain't lucky enough to live up there on Venus, Cleano is the real cleaning stuff!"

Then the chorus went into their "Cleano-is-the-stuff" jingle, but Mrs. Garvy didn't hear it. She was a stubborn woman, but it occurred to her that she was very sick indeed. She didn't want to worry her husband. The next day she quietly made an appointment with her family freud.

In the waiting room she picked up a fresh new copy of *Readers Pablum* and put it down with a faint palpitation. The lead article, according to the table of contents on the cover, was titled "The Most Memorable Venusian I Ever Met."

"The freud will see you now," said the nurse, and Mrs. Garvy tottered into his office.

His traditional glasses and whiskers were reassuring. She choked out the ritual. "Freud, forgive me, for I have neuroses."

He chanted the antiphonal, "Tut, my dear girl, what seems to be the trouble?"

"I got like a hole in the head," she quavered. "I seem to forget all kinds of things. Things like everybody seems to know and I don't."

"Well, that happens to everybody occasionally, my dear. I suggest a vacation on Venus."

The freud stared, openmouthed, at the empty chair. His nurse came in and demanded, "Hey, you see how she scrammed? What was the matter with *her?*"

He took off his glasses and whiskers meditatively. "You can search me. I told her she should maybe try a vacation on Venus." A momentary bafflement came into his face and he dug through his desk drawers until he found a copy of the four-color, profusely illustrated journal of his profession. It had come that morning and he had lip-read it, though looking mostly at the pictures. He leafed to the article "Advantages of the Planet Venus in Rest Cures."

"It's right there," he said.

The nurse looked. "It sure is," she agreed. "Why shouldn't it be?"

"The trouble with these here neurotics," decided the freud, "is that they all the time got to fight reality. Show in the next twitch."

He put on his glasses and whiskers again and forgot Mrs. Garvy and her strange behavior.

"Freud, forgive me, for I have neuroses."

"Tut, my dear girl, what seems to be the trouble?"

Like many cures of mental disorders, Mrs. Garvy's was achieved largely by self-treatment. She disciplined herself sternly out of the crazy notion that there had been only one rocket ship and that one a failure. She could join without wincing, eventually, in any conversation on the desirability of Venus as a place to retire, on its fabulous floral profusion. Finally she went to Venus.

All her friends were trying to book passage with the Evening Star Travel and Real Estate Corporation, but naturally the demand was crushing. She considered herself lucky to get a seat at last for the two-week summer cruise. The spaceship took off from a place called Los Alamos, New Mexico. It looked just like all the spaceships on television and in the picture magazines but was more comfortable than you would expect.

Mrs. Garvy was delighted with the fifty or so fellow-passengers assembled before takeoff. They were from all over the country and she had a distinct impression that they were on the brainy side. The captain, a tall, hawk-faced, impressive fellow named Ryan Something-or-other, welcomed them aboard and trusted that their trip would be a memorable one. He regretted that there would be nothing to see because, "due to the meteorite season," the ports would be dogged down. It was disappointing, yet reassuring that the line was taking no chances.

There was the expected momentary discomfort at takeoff and then two monotonous days of droning travel through space to be whiled away in the lounge at cards or craps. The landing was a routine bump and the voyagers were issued tablets to swallow to immunize them against any minor ailments.

When the tablets took effect, the lock was opened, and Venus was theirs.

It looked much like a tropical island on Earth, except for a blanket of cloud overhead. But it had a heady, otherworldly quality that was intoxicating and glamorous.

The ten days of the vacation were suffused with a hazy magic. The soap root, as advertised, was free and sudsy. The fruits, mostly tropical varieties transplanted from Earth, were delightful. The simple shelters provided by the travel company were more than adequate for the balmy days and nights.

It was with sincere regret that the voyagers filed again into the ship and swallowed more tablets doled out to counteract and sterilize any Venus illnesses they might unwittingly communicate to Earth.

Vacationing was one thing. Power politics was another.

At the Pole, a small man was in a soundproof room, his face deathly pale and his body limp in a straight chair.

In the American Senate Chamber, Senator Hull-Mendoza (Synd., N. Cal.) was saying, "Mr. President and gentlemen, I would be remiss in my duty as a legislature if'n I didn't bring to the attention of the au-gust body I see here a perilous situation which is fraught with peril. As is well known to members of this au-gust body, the perfection of space flight has brought with it a situation I can only describe as fraught with peril. Mr. President and gentlemen, now that swift American rockets now traverse the trackless void of space between this planet and our nearest planetarial neighbor in space—and, gentlemen, I refer to Venus, the star of dawn, the brightest jewel in fair Vulcan's diadome—now, I say, I want to inquire what steps are being taken to colonize Venus with a vanguard of patriotic citizens like those minutemen of yore.

"Mr. President and gentlemen! There are in this world nations, envious nations—I do not name Mexico—who by fair means or foul may seek to wrest from Columbia's grasp the torch of freedom of space; nations whose low living standards and innate depravity give them an unfair advantage over the citizens of our fair republic.

"This is my program: I suggest that a city of more than 100,-000 population be selected by lot. The citizens of the fortunate city are to be awarded choice lands on Venus free and clear, to have and to hold and convey to their descendants. And the national government shall provide free transportation to Venus for these citizens. And this program shall continue, city by city, until there has been deposited on Venus a sufficient vanguard of citizens to protect our manifest rights in that planet.

"Objections will be raised, for carping critics we have always with us. They will say there isn't enough steel. They will call it a cheap giveaway. I say there *is* enough steel for *one* city's population to be transferred to Venus, and that is all that is needed. For when the time comes for the second city to be transferred, the first, emptied city can be wrecked for the needed steel! And is it a giveaway? Yes! It is the most glorious giveaway in the history of mankind! Mr. President and gentlemen, there is no time to waste—Venus must be American!"

Black-Kupperman, at the Pole, opened his eyes and said feebly, "The style was a little uneven. Do you think anybody'll notice?"

"You did fine, boy; just fine," Barlow reassured him.

Hull-Mendoza's bill became law.

Drafting machines at the South Pole were busy around the clock and the Pittsburgh steel mills spewed millions of plates into the Los Alamos spaceport of the Evening Star Travel and Real Estate Corporation. It was going to be Los Angeles, for logistic reasons, and the three most accomplished psychokineticists went to Washington and mingled in the crowd at the drawing to make certain that the Los Angeles capsule slithered into the fingers of the blindfolded Senator.

Los Angeles loved the idea and a forest of spaceships began to blossom in the desert. They weren't very good spaceships, but they didn't have to be.

A team at the Pole worked at Barlow's direction on a mail setup. There would have to be letters to and from Venus to keep the slightest taint of suspicion from arising. Luckily Barlow remembered that the problem had been solved once before —by Hitler. Relatives of persons incinerated in the furnaces of Lublin or Majdanek continued to get cheery postal cards.

The Los Angeles flight went off on schedule, under tremendous press, newsreel and television coverage. The world cheered the gallant Angelenos who were setting off on their patriotic voyage to the land of milk and honey. The forest of spaceships

thundered up, and up, and out of sight without untoward inci
dent. Billions envied the Angelenos, cramped and on short ra
tions though they were.

Wreckers from San Francisco, whose capsule came up sec
ond, moved immediately into the city of the angels for the scra
steel their own flight would require. Senator Hull-Mendoza
constituents could do no less.

The president of Mexico, hypnotically alarmed at this exten
sion of *yanqui imperialismo* beyond the stratosphere, launche
his own Venus-colony program.

Across the water it was England versus Ireland, France ver
sus Germany, China versus Russia, India versus Indonesia. An
cient hatreds grew into the flames that were rocket ships assai
ing the air by hundreds daily.

Dear Ed, how are you? Sam and I are fine and hope you
are fine. Is it nice up there like they say with food and
close grone on trees? I drove by Springfield yesterday and
it sure looked funny all the buildings down but of coarse
it is worth it we have to keep the greasers in their place.
Do you have any truble with them on Venus? Drop me a
line some time. Your loving sister, Alma.

Dear Alma, I am fine and hope you are fine. It is a fine
place here fine climate and easy living. The doctor told me
today that I seem to be ten years younger. He thinks there
is something in the air here keeps people young. We do
not have much trouble with the greasers here they keep to
theirselves it is just a question of us outnumbering them
and staking out the best places for the Americans. In
South Bay I know a nice little island that I have been sav-
ing for you and Sam with lots of blanket trees and ham
bushes. Hoping to see you and Sam soon, your loving
brother, Ed.

Sam and Alma were on their way shortly.

Poprob got a dividend in every nation after the emigration had passed the halfway mark. The lonesome stay-at-homes were unable to bear the melancholy of a low population density; their conditioning had been to swarms of their kin. After that point it was possible to foist off the crudest stripped-down accommodations on would-be emigrants; they didn't care.

Black-Kupperman did a final job on President Hull-Mendoza, the last job that genius of hypnotics would ever do on any moron, important or otherwise.

Hull-Mendoza, panic stricken by his presidency over an emptying nation, joined his constituents. The *Independence*, aboard which traveled the national government of America, was the most elaborate of all the spaceships—bigger, more comfortable, with a lounge that was handsome, though cramped, and cloakrooms for Senators and Representatives. It went, however, to the same place as the others and Black-Kupperman killed himself, leaving a note that stated he "couldn't live with my conscience."

The day after the American President departed, Barlow flew into a rage. Across his specially built desk were supposed to flow all Poprob high-level documents, and this thing—this outrageous thing—called Poprob*term* apparently had got into the executive stage before he had even had a glimpse of it!

He buzzed for Rogge-Smith, his statistician. Rogge-Smith seemed to be at the bottom of it. Poprobterm seemed to be about first and second and third derivatives, whatever they were. Barlow had a deep distrust of anything more complex than what he called an "average."

While Rogge-Smith was still at the door, Barlow snapped, "What's the meaning of this? Why haven't I been consulted? How far have you people got and why have you been working on something I haven't authorized?"

"Didn't want to bother you, Chief," said Rogge-Smith. "It

was really a technical matter, kind of a final cleanup. Want to come and see the work?"

Mollified, Barlow followed his statistician down the corridor.

"You still shouldn't have gone ahead without my okay," he grumbled. "Where the hell would you people have been without me?"

"That's right, Chief. We couldn't have swung it ourselves; our minds just don't work that way. And all that stuff you knew from Hitler—it wouldn't have occurred to us. Like poor Black-Kupperman."

They were in a fair-sized machine shop at the end of a slight upward incline. It was cold. Rogge-Smith pushed a button that started a motor, and a flood of arctic light poured in as the roof parted slowly. It showed a small spaceship with the door open.

Barlow gaped as Rogge-Smith took him by the elbow and his other boys appeared: Swenson-Swenson, the engineer; Tsutsu-gimushi-Duncan, his propellants man; Kalb-French, advertising.

"In you go, Chief," said Tsutsugimushi-Duncan. "This is Poprobterm."

"But I'm the world Dictator!"

"You bet, Chief. You'll be in history, all right—but this is necessary, I'm afraid."

The door was closed. Acceleration slammed Barlow cruelly to the metal floor. Something broke, and warm, wet stuff, salty tasting, ran from his mouth to his chin. Arctic sunlight through a port suddenly became a fierce lancet stabbing at his eyes; he was out of the atmosphere.

Lying twisted and broken under the acceleration, Barlow realized that some things had not changed, that Jack Ketch was never asked to dinner however many shillings you paid him to do your dirty work, that murder will out, that crime pays only temporarily.

The last thing he learned was that death is the end of pain.

Leo P. Kelley

THE MYTHMASTER

She was wandering aimlessly down the steps of the building, her eyes focused on distant lands, her pale hands folded in front of her like those of a polite schoolgirl who knows the teacher is looking.

The man approached her. He released the trigger of his glowgas gun and left a harmless identifying mark on the girl's forehead. It would disappear in time. And she might never know that she had been violated. His victims often did not realize that they were pregnant. These unknowing ones were lucky, because they had not learned that they had a child to lose—and had lost it to the Mythmaster.

He was a pirate of the lowest sort—he stole human lives. And the most powerful criminal in the starlanes wanted to own him—and the woman he hated.

Also by Leo P. Kelley

THE MAN FROM MAYBE

The lost memory, the computerised harem of Superstud, the flight from the dreaded Marsman . . .

You lose your memory; and you find a new lifestyle.

You seem to lose sexuality; and you find a new type of lust.

You lose your sense of time; and you find time re-paced and re-defined.

You search for yourself; and you meet 'Helen of Troy' and 'Professor Apocalypse'.

You read this book; and you are taken into worlds that are frightening and unknown.

Also by Leo P. Kelley

THE COINS OF MURPH

Toss the coin; toss the coin; toss the coin—and travel through Time with the aid of Chance.

Beforeit became Afterit and Afterit shall never be the same as Beforeit. For once Mankind made decisions; and Murph has ordered a change in the ways of man.

The wheels of Murph grind slowly, but exceedingly small; and Randland waits for the Losers. But once the Toss has been Lost and Murph's power has been questioned—then shall the need to voyage through Afterit become more important, and the power of the Coins be diminished.

A SELECTION FROM SOME OF CORONET'S LEADING SCI-FI WRITERS: